Some Die Young

Also by Jeanne Hart

Fetish

Some Die Young

A Carl Pedersen Mystery

Jeanne Hart

St. Martin's Press · New York

Library of Congress Cataloging-in-Publication Data

Hart, Jeanne.
   Some die young.
      p.   cm.
   "A Thomas Dunne book."
   ISBN 0-312-03936-0
   I. Title.
PS3558.A6816S66   1990   813'.54—dc20   89-24338

First Edition
10 9 8 7 6 5 4 3 2 1

To my children, Tina, Amy, and Mark
and to the memory of
their father, Jules Schrager

1

Meredith Crane closed her bedroom door, sat down at her white painted desk and opened her new diary. Really, it was not a diary: the blank pages had no dates. But it was bound in red-orange leather that was silky to the touch and was big enough that she wouldn't have to cramp her writing. She ran a finger over the smooth cover, picked up the new black felt-tipped pen and opened the book to the first page. She felt new, like the journal, like the pen, as though turning twelve years old were a beginning.

Thursday, March 17

Today is my twelfth birthday and I've decided something. I'm going to be like Anne Frank. Not hiding from the Nazis or dying, but a writer like her. She started with a diary and I'm going to do the same thing. Lisa writes poetry and Jennifer dances, and this is going to be the thing I'll do. This diary—my mother says I should call it a journal—was given to me by Mother. Actually, the card

said, "Love from Sean and Mother," but I know it was
really from my mother.

The thing about this birthday is that certain things I was
sure would happen to me by now still haven't. I still . . .

As she wrote, she smiled to herself, aware she was smiling. When, finally, she closed the book, she had five solid blocks of writing. It was a start. She stood for a moment, undecided, and then walked across the room and slipped it between her mattress and the box springs of her bed. Sean was not likely to go snooping there. If—she thought back to what she had written about him—if he'd even bother to snoop these days.

She went out of the room still smiling and closed the door behind her.

2

The girl was reported missing at nine forty-five Friday evening. Until then her parents continued to assume she would show up.

Lisa Margolin had always been an independent child. Both parents worked, and she was often on her own for several hours after school. She hiked and bicycled and sat on the rocks above the water. Her two closest friends were Meredith Crane and Jennifer Johnson, Meredith being the closer friend because their mothers worked together, which made her like family. Usually when her parents returned to find Lisa out, there was a note saying she was having dinner with one or the other of those friends. It struck them as odd, forgetful, that she had left no note that Friday, but she had been home: a new poem was affixed to the refrigerator with a magnet. Her bicycle was gone; she had not taken her dog, Taffy, as she never did when she biked.

Nonetheless, they checked. The Cranes were out. Jennifer Johnson was in, but she had not seen Lisa since school that afternoon. She thought Lisa was probably somewhere with the Cranes; she hadn't spoken with Meredith for a couple of days, but she had noticed her talking to Lisa when she left for dance class.

"It's all right," said Jean Margolin, hanging up. "Lisa's somewhere with Meredith. But I'm going to have a thing or two to say to that young lady when she does come in." Jean seldom spoke that way; it occurred to her that what she said sounded more like her mother speaking than herself. She went to the kitchen to feed Taffy, normally Lisa's job.

Jean and Pete had a leisurely dinner—an omelette, since it was just the two of them, and a glass of wine, which they seldom served unless they were entertaining. It was rather nice being by themselves for a change, although there was a mild unease. Several times conversation faltered: they were abstracted, although not truly anxious.

In fact, they did not become actively worried until shortly before nine. Lisa knew she was to call or be in by nine. At the same moment, they stood up from where they sat reading. "Let's try the Cranes again," said Pete Margolin. He picked up the receiver to dial.

"Oh, my God." Jean Margolin's legs suddenly wobbled beneath her. "I *forgot*. The Cranes have gone up to Sonoma County for the weekend. She *can't* be with them." She took the phone from her husband, her eyes wide. "Could she be at Mother's?" Her mother lived ten miles south, on the bus line.

Her mother was indignant. "No, she's not here. Of course not. Lisa would never come way down here without my letting you know. Have you called the police?"

"No." Jean tried to keep the terror that was rising in her from her voice. If she let go, she knew in a moment her mother would be hysterical. "It seems so—extreme, calling the police, but I'm really worried now. I was sure she was with the Cranes. But don't worry, Mother, you know Lisa; she never bikes anywhere there aren't lots of people, and she knows not to go with strangers or get into cars. It's just that I can't for the life of me think where she can be."

"Well, she's not here." In a gentler voice, her mother added,

4

"Maybe she fell or something, Jean. Broke her leg and can't get home."

"But where? Everywhere she goes there are people."

"It rained down here this afternoon. Didn't it there?"

"Yes, it's raining now."

"There wouldn't be any people around if it's raining."

"That's true." Jean sounded doubtful. "We"—she hesitated— "haven't called the hospitals. Maybe we should."

"Try them and call me back. I'll be right here by the phone."

But neither of Bay Cove's hospitals had admitted Lisa. A call to each of three emergency walk-in clinics yielded no more. Methodically, aware of the cold stillness that was growing within them, Jean and Pete combed through Lisa's address book and called acquaintances. Nothing. By the time Jean put down the phone after the last call, Pete was in his raincoat. "I'm going to the police. You stay here in case she gets in touch. Give me that picture of her from the bookcase." He stuffed it in his pocket, not looking at it.

Jean stood in the open doorway watching his car disappear around the corner. She craned to either side, her eyes filled with the bicycle and the girl that she did not see. Going indoors, she walked back to Lisa's room. In her clothes closet, everything was as usual; only the green waterproof jacket was missing. She must have taken it when she stopped off home. Jean ran a hand over the stack of schoolbooks piled on the desk. It was comforting to think she *had* been there.

The police were not reassuring. The officer, who looked so young it seemed doubtful that he had yet shaved, noted the facts, inquired about family disputes, and, although clearly he had concluded before Pete began to speak that here was another runaway, patiently listened to Pete's protestation that Lisa was not that sort of child. Young as the officer was, he had heard it all before. "We'll get on it," he said. "The best thing you can do, sir, is stay close to the phone. Let me know when you

5

hear from your daughter." Pete picked up the unspoken, *if you hear.* He turned away, suddenly spent.

Jean met him at the door. "Anything?"

"No, I've looked everywhere. *Everywhere.* The police took the information." On the way home the thought had kept going through Pete's mind that perhaps Lisa *had* run away. Children had secret lives their parents knew nothing about. Perhaps he and Jean didn't know their daughter at all. He mentioned nothing of the thought to Jean.

"I'm cold," Jean said. She was trembling, her teeth chattering. "I can't get warm. I'm so cold."

"I'll turn up the heat." When he turned from the thermostat, Jean saw for the first time how white he was. Her own face felt rigid, the skin stretched tight. They seated themselves to wait, apart, as though they were afraid to touch.

A creak of the floor, a door blown open by the storm, a sudden heavier spatter of rain—each brought them to their feet, hopeful. They did not sleep.

And Lisa did not return.

3

The rain let up late Monday morning, shortly before the body was found.

Pedersen and Tate were sent out on the call. In his office, Detective-Sergeant Pedersen was picturing a hamburger oozing with juices and topped by a thick slice of onion at just about the point at which Lieutenant Harbison called him in.

"Carl, that kid's been found. Dead. In Richards West. I want you and Ron to get over there."

Pedersen was aware that he wasn't responding.

"Carl, you hear me?"

"The missing girl?"

"Yes, the twelve-year-old. Found in Richards West Park, stuffed under some shrubbery. Apparently raped and strangled."

"You need me—"

"Yes. *You*. Carl, I know this isn't pleasant. I want you and Ron on it. Get on over there." He stood up and slammed his fist hard on his desk. "*Fuck* those perverts! A *twelve*-year-old!" He had a ten-year-old daughter.

Such an outburst from the normally circumspect Harbison, who seldom raised his voice and never uttered even a mild oath, startled Pedersen and brought him to attention. He hated crimes involving children, hated them. Harbison knew it. But then, every man on the force hated them.

Detective Tate, his partner, was as gloomy as he at the prospect. They rode wordlessly the several blocks to the park. Richards West was a public park, near enough the center of town to be popular: its water exercise classes and swim groups continued through the winter in the heated outdoor pool; its picnic tables and playing fields were alive with families and noisy ball players all week year round; and its recreation hall was in constant demand. Not heavily wooded, nonetheless it had paths verdant with trees and bushes and little coves and corners along the river in which one could have the illusion that one was alone. One seldom was, however, which made it a strange choice as a murder site.

A small crowd had gathered to gape. The patrol officer stood with his partner, awkwardly shooing them back. Pedersen could see that it was as distasteful to Muller and Geberth as to himself that people should gawk at the murder of a child, whispering and staring. He pulled up and jumped from the car. "Be sure the crime scene boys are on their way," he said over his shoulder to Tate. "Let's get on this and get her out of here." He strode to where the gawkers clustered. "This isn't a circus, you know." He started moving them back from the scene, his face dark with fury. The crowd quieted and retreated, frightened or shamed by his anger.

He turned and plunged into the park. The girl had been taken—coaxed, with what ruse?—along the path into the wooded area and from there into a green cove out of sight of park activities. The small body—she was a small twelve-year-old, blonde, thin, rather frail looking—lay pushed back under heavy, enveloping bushes. Despite the cramped posture, her jeans and panties had been partially pulled back up over her hips. Pedersen bent over the body. The marks of strangu-

8

lation were dark on her throat. The body did not look fresh. The cold rain of the past weekend had softened the ground around her; the bushes had to some extent sheltered her from the rain, but her clothes were soaked through. He stood looking down at her. Was it the green jacket that kept her from being spotted earlier? Or had the rain that had come down steadily all weekend made the search more superficial than it should have been? He sighed and stepped back.

Howard Rand, the coroner's deputy, was working in another part of town; by the time he arrived, the crime-scene team had gathered all material possible without touching the corpse. Rand rose from his examination of the body with some surprise. "Been here all weekend, I'd say. Hard to imagine she wouldn't be found in that time in a place like this."

"The rain. Nobody's been using the park."

"I suppose. Wasn't anybody looking for her?"

"Yes. Her parents reported her missing late Friday night. We should have found her way before this."

"Well. You can have her taken away as soon as they're done here. Looks like a simple case of strangulation."

Simple, Pedersen thought. How these people think.

He glanced once more at the green-clad little body, which, except for the dark marks on the throat—the purpling of the face had faded—might otherwise have crawled under a bush out of the weather.

Back at the car, he said to Tate, "With all this rain, it's going to be hard coming up with anything."

"Yes. Do you know who she was?"

"I know she's the daughter of some people who live over on Willow. He works for the university; the mother works for *Intermission*."

"That arts magazine?"

"Yes. The father apparently came into headquarters all upset Friday night, sure she hadn't run away and that something had happened to her. I wasn't there; Pillegi told me about it. Apparently the kid was on her own a lot when they were at work, and they didn't get worried till nearly nine, when she didn't show up at her curfew hour. They called around to some friends, and then he came down to headquarters." He looked toward the scene of the crime. "Her bike must have been stolen; she was biking. Probably she left it under a tree, and someone came along and saw a good thing."

"I can't see how they missed her when they went through the park."

"I gather they were concentrating on the bay shore area. Sent a dive team, did a water search, but nothing showed up. Her parents said she liked to go down there near the lighthouse, watch the surfers."

"At night?"

"No, but they figured she might have gone there after school. In fact, the general consensus, Harbison said, was that the kid had fallen off a rock, drowned."

"Maybe a surfer killed her. Cute little girl hanging around."

"A little *too* little for it to be just anybody. Only certain kinds go for twelve-year-olds."

Tate did not comment on that. They continued to wait, each busy with his own thoughts.

4

"I blame myself," the woman said. "I blame only myself." Lisa Margolin's mother had herself under rigid control, except for a tic in one eye that kept pulsing and which she kept trying to brush away.

"Now, Jean," her husband said. He sounded weary of making that particular protest.

"No, it's true, Pete." They had just returned from the morgue; she turned to the detective who sat opposite her in the large living room. Sun shone through the clean, uncurtained panes and lighted the brilliant colors in the Navajo rug. The woman sat on the edge of a white linen-covered couch, which looked soft and comfortable. She looked only at her hands in her lap, as though an acknowledgment of the room and its color would be a desecration. "I work," she explained. "I work, and I've tried to make Lisa independent. She's—was—an only child; only children become independent early, anyway. But apparently I didn't teach her caution. I *thought* I did; I told her all the things you tell children, but—"

"Jean, stop talking. Let go and cry." He had; his eyes were swollen almost shut.

She flung a furious glance at him.

He sighed. "Jean, we couldn't anticipate everything. *You* couldn't. You don't know what he did or said to get her to go with him." He looked exhausted.

"That's true, Mrs. Margolin," Pedersen said. "These men are clever. They're persuasive."

"I just can't believe—" She turned her head away.

"What we need to know is something about Lisa's habits, something that might give us a direction to follow. You said she spent a lot of time down by the water watching the surfers. Do you suppose she'd have gone off with one of them?"

"No," said Pete Margolin.

"How can we know who she went off with?" said Jean Margolin bitterly. "It could have been anybody."

"Did she ever mention talking to a surfer or getting acquainted with any of them?"

"No," she said. "I don't think it was a surfer."

"How did she get to the water usually? She always biked?"

"Most of the time. Once in a while she took the dog and walked, but usually she biked. Her bike is gone."

"Yes. It hasn't been found. And the park, was that one of her—haunts?"

"Not that I'm aware of. She went there to swim now and then—they have after-school swim hours. You have to be under eighteen to use the pool at that time. She went there sometimes."

"Maybe Meredith would know," Pete said. "Or Jennifer."

"Friends?" Pedersen asked.

She nodded. "Yes. They might know if Lisa had been"—she could barely get the words out—"meeting anyone."

"You think she may have been?"

"I don't think anything. Not anything." With a jerk, she turned her head away.

"Jean," her husband protested. "But"—he addressed the detective—"you should talk to them. They might have a clue, if she was up to anything."

12

Pedersen jotted down the addresses. "Now if we could see her room—"

"Yes," said Jean briskly. "It's down the hall here. The dog is in there." For the first time her eyes filled. "He misses her. He knows something is wrong."

The room told them little. It revealed the same hand that had decorated the living room. A Mexican throw rug with a vertical pattern of dark blue birds lay on the floor; the bed was covered with a Guatemalan fabric. The room was tidy, schoolbooks piled neatly on the desk, clothes hung away. In one corner in a shallow, battered Mexican basket, a small dog was curled. It lifted its head as they entered and then returned its head to its paws, following them with its eyes. A comfortable upholstered chair sat in another corner next to a floor lamp. A book with a bookmark in it lay on the chair. Pedersen picked it up. It was *Flowers for Algernon*.

"Did she keep a diary?"

"No, nothing of that sort. She wrote poetry, though. She left a poem on the refrigerator for us when she went out Friday. I'll get it."

She returned. The poem was brief:

> Silver-toed
> the waves kick at the shore
> determined to have their way.

Tate raised his eyebrows. "That's very nice," he said.

"She liked haiku. And William Carlos Williams." She began to cry. "She was such a—such a—"

"We can see that, Mrs. Margolin," Pedersen said. "An unusual girl."

"Yes," she said gratefully, fishing in her pocket for a tissue. "She *was* unusual. It's such a *waste*."

At her tears, the dog climbed out of its basket and came over to her, sniffing at her ankles. She bent down to stroke him. "Taffy will miss her so. She adored Taffy and Taffy adored her." Blindly she turned to leave the room. "You look at her room. I'll be—in here."

13

After she had gone, Pedersen said, "This kid was disciplined. Look at the condition of the room. Not like most twelve-year-olds' bedrooms."

Tate was examining the titles on the crowded bookshelves, the long, lean, bespectacled figure in the corduroy jacket intent. "I didn't see a TV anywhere around, did you?"

"No. And none in here. This family paid attention. Funny she could have been taken in."

"Her reading is mostly adult books. Odd. She looked like such a little girl."

"That's her build. Like her mother—slim, no breasts to speak of." He was sorting through the papers in her desk drawer.

Tate searched the dresser. "Nothing here," he said. "No hidden stashes of dope or birth control pills or any of those little surprises we usually come on."

"Not much here, either." Pedersen turned over a letter he was reading. "She started this letter to a friend, let's see, a week ago, but it's all perfectly innocuous stuff." He sighed. "I guess we'd better get over to the girl friends' houses. We're not going to learn anything here."

Tate said from the clothes closet, "Jeans, shirts, sweaters, a raincoat. Nothing in the pockets except tissues." He hung up a terry-cloth robe he had been checking. "Did the letter say *anything?*"

"Nothing. The dog had been to the vet. Stuff like that. No cigarettes around. She seems to have been an ideal daughter, did just what her parents had in mind for her."

"Except this once."

"Well, we don't know. We have no idea what he did to get her to go with him. She may have thought she was doing the right thing."

"She wouldn't have fallen for that 'Your parents sent me' routine. A girl doing this kind of reading would have been too sophisticated."

"I didn't mean that," Pedersen said. "That's not what I meant."

T hey had phoned ahead. Jennifer was home from school. Her mother met them at the door, a regal-looking coffee-colored woman. "Now, look," she said, her voice lowered. "I

14

don't want you upsetting Jennifer. She's upset enough. Try to put things so she won't be—"

"We'll be as gentle as possible, Mrs. Johnson," Pedersen said. "We just want to know if she can give us any leads."

"I don't see how. But come in."

The house was grander than the Margolins' and more conventionally furnished, but it had a color and warmth that was welcoming. Jennifer stood up politely as they entered. She was going to be a beauty like her mother. Her carriage was remarkable and she looked a good four years older than Lisa. She had been crying.

Mrs. Johnson indicated chairs.

"Jennifer," Pedersen said, "We know this whole thing has been disturbing to you, but we need to ask you just a few things. Questions to which maybe only you know the answers."

Her eyes were appraising. "What sort of questions?"

"First of all, may I ask how old you are?"

"Thirteen in November, but I entered school a year later than Lisa, so we're in the same grade." She raised her eyes to his. "I know I look older."

"You do. I wondered."

"She's studied dance since she was five. Dancers have good carriage," Mrs. Johnson said.

Pedersen smiled. "I noticed. Now, Jennifer, first of all, was Lisa as young as she looked? You know what I mean, was she naïve, innocent to the point where she might easily have been—"

"Conned? No, she wasn't that young. She just looked that way. She and I were pretty much the same. I wouldn't call Lisa naïve."

"Was she—into anything her parents didn't know about?"

Mrs. Johnson rose. "I think this conversation would go more smoothly with me out of the room. I have some things to take care of upstairs. Let me know when you're ready to leave." As an afterthought, she added, "I didn't offer you anything. Would you like a cup of coffee?"

"No, thank you, we're fine." They heard her mother mounting the stairs. "What about that, Jennifer? Drugs? Boys? Things she concealed from her parents?" He glanced at her. "You aren't being disloyal if you tell us. It may help us find her killer."

Jennifer laughed suddenly, a sharp little sound. "Adults are all alike. You always think we're leading wild secret lives. Lisa wasn't into anything like that. Neither of us. Drugs are dumb, we know better, and as for boys, she kind of liked one boy in our math class, but he never asked her out, and from the looks of him, he was more scared than she was. I," she said thoughtfully, "would be more likely to be involved with boys. But," she went on, "I'm not. I just mean I'm more"—her face darkened slightly in a flush—"what you'd call more ready, I guess. No, somebody fooled her. I can't believe she'd fall for that sort of thing, but that's what must have happened. My mother really needn't have gone upstairs."

"I can see that," Pedersen said. "Now let's talk about Friday, the day she was killed." He saw the girl wince. "I'm sorry, but I must. Tell me whether anything unusual happened at school."

"No, nothing. I had a dance class to go to. Lisa said something about a walk. She was going to stop off for a raincoat. When I left, she was talking to Meredith."

"Her schoolbooks were on her table, but she didn't pick up a raincoat," Tate said. "She was wearing jeans and a green jacket."

"That green jacket's waterproof. And long. It wasn't raining hard yet, I suppose she thought that was enough. It has a hood."

"Where would you have expected her to go for her walk?"

"Over to the water. But I wasn't surprised she was found in the park. She biked there pretty often. There's a nice little path along the river. She used to sit on the bank and"—she hesitated—"you know about the poetry?"

"Her mother showed us a very nice poem she wrote," Tate said. "She left it on the refrigerator when she stopped off at home Friday. She must have written it at school."

"Yes." Jennifer smiled faintly. "She's been known to write a poem when she should be working on math or science." Her eyes filled. "I'm going to miss her. I could—tell her things. My mother says it's because our values are the same."

"Obviously you are—were—both mature for your age,"

16

Pedersen said. She looked pleased. "If you were going to try to lure a person like Lisa off into the woods, what method would you use?"

Her answer came immediately. "I'd tell her my dog was hurt. Or hers."

Pedersen and Tate looked at each other.

"That's very perceptive," said Tate.

"She loved Taffy. I'm not so crazy about animals myself, I guess because I never had a pet, but she was really a little soft in the head when it came to animals. I used to tell her the Save the Whales people really needed her. She didn't think it was funny."

"That's very helpful," Pedersen said. "Now have we covered everything? There isn't anything you want to tell us that we haven't thought to ask? Her school grades hadn't fallen off lately, anything like that?"

"No. Lisa was a wonderful person, wonderful. I can't see how anybody could have"—her voice dipped huskily, and she stood up. "I'll tell my mother you're going."

As she climbed the stairs to get her mother, Pedersen looked around. "No TV here, either."

"No. Same values, remember?"

"I remember. That's one articulate kid."

Tate smiled gently. "That's what no TV does."

"Mmm," said Pedersen absently. "You realize, if he did use that ploy, the hurt dog, he must have been following her around observing her for a while?"

"Or else he knew her," said Tate.

T he other friend was wary. Wary and uneasy. Meredith Crane and her brother Sean were alone in the apartment, perhaps that was one reason. Mrs. Johnson had, despite withdrawing from the interview, provided a sort of buffer for Jennifer. No such buffer was present for Meredith, unless her unkempt, scornful teenaged brother could have been considered one.

Pedersen opened his identification folder. "We phoned. Your mother isn't here?"

"No." She glanced at her brother. "Sean's eighteen."

"I see. Guess you'll have to act as chaperon then, Sean. That all right with you?"

The boy nodded doubtfully.

"Come in," the girl said. She led them into the living room. It was a big room lined with books, floor to ceiling, with a sliding ladder to provide access to the highest books.

"It's a library," Tate remarked with pleasure, "a real library." He was the son of a librarian.

"Yes, well," Meredith said, "my grandfather died and we inherited all his books, on top of all ours. Mother had to do something."

Pedersen wondered if they had inherited the huge Turkish rug as well. And the long sofa upholstered in rich brown leather. The room had a look of luxury that did not square with the salary of a minor editor of an insignificant local arts magazine. Meredith appeared to have read his mind. "Almost everything in here was Grandpa's. The rest of the house is just—ordinary."

Her brother laughed.

She looked at the two detectives. "You came to ask me questions about Lisa."

"We did. What can you tell me about her, Meredith?"

"I—what do you want to know? She was my friend." She leaned forward. She looked frightened. "Do you know who killed her? Have you an idea?"

"Some freak," her brother said.

"Like you," she said and then blushed deeply. "I didn't mean that."

He shrugged. "No skin off my ass. I think you're pretty weird, too."

Pedersen took things in hand. "First tell me," he said, "whether there was anything going on in her life that her family didn't know about. Don't worry about confidences—this has nothing to do with that. It has to do with finding a murderer."

18

She slid away from him, further back in her chair. "When you say it like that . . ."

"That's the way it is, Meredith. Now what about that?"

"She didn't"—she threw an uneasy glance in her brother's direction—"do drugs or anything like that. Is that what you mean?"

"What about a boyfriend?"

Sean laughed again, contemptuously.

She ignored him. "No-o-o. A couple weeks ago our mothers took us up to the *Intermission* offices to meet some of the people and to see how magazines are run; Lisa liked one of the men there, she talked about him a lot, but that was just a—crush. She didn't have a real boyfriend."

"She liked one of the men?"

"I mean—she said afterwards that she thought he was . . . I don't know, something. Pretty special or something like that." In a great rush, she added, "She liked a boy in our math class. But I think—" She left the sentence uncompleted.

"Tell me about the man."

"I shouldn't have said that. She just *admired* him. I didn't mean that she went out with him or anything like that. Like I said, it was a crush. He wouldn't go out with *us*."

"What was his name, Meredith?"

She looked really frightened now. "I don't remember." It was clear she did.

"If Lisa talked about him, you must recall his name."

"I don't." She set her chin stubbornly. She was built rather like Lisa, small and as yet unformed, but a future prettiness hung over her like a veil. With her bright hair—when she was littler, she must have been dubbed Carrot Top—her brown eyes and high color, she would be vivid, exciting: she would have to fight off the men.

He studied the determined little face. "For the moment, let's let that go. Tell me if anything at all out of the ordinary happened Friday. If she said anything, did anything different from the usual. Did she mention meeting anyone, for example?"

"She just said she was going for a walk. Lisa liked to walk in the rain. She was a very—romantic girl."

19

Pedersen wondered if she meant *romantic* in the sense in which he understood it. "She wrote poetry. Did she show it to you?"

"Yes. Lots."

"Did she write about anyone? Think back, was there a hint of friendship with someone in her poetry?"

"With a boy, you mean?"

"A boy. Or a man."

She had remembered something, but had decided not to tell, Pedersen was sure. "No," she said. "Mostly they were poems about nature. And Taffy. And she wrote one for her parents' anniversary."

"And you haven't recalled the name of that man Lisa admired? You understand why I'm asking?"

"Yes. I don't remember, but if I did I wouldn't tell you. Why should I get somebody who's perfectly *innocent* in trouble?"

"He may not be innocent."

"Oh, really." With a flounce, she got to her feet. "He probably didn't even know Lisa existed, I mean once we left the magazine. Grown-ups—adults, I mean, don't pay attention to people twelve years old."

She had a point; it was just that she didn't understand about pedophiles. "Anything else you want to tell me?"

"No. I think you should go. If you want to talk to me some more, I think you should come back when my mother's here."

"*I'm* here," said Sean, with mock expansiveness.

"Oh, you," she said.

For a moment, a look of pain slipped across his face. Then he laughed.

Thank God my kids didn't get along like that, Pedersen thought as they left the building. He realized he hadn't taken the name of the boy in math class.

5

Meredith Crane closed the bedroom door with a bang. Her brother had just said something extremely rude to her, and she was not about to remain in the same room with him. Angrily, she tugged at the mattress and retrieved her journal. Her mother would be home soon, expecting her to set the table and help make salad, but now she could take a little time for writing.

Before she began to write, she read over the last paragraphs of her first entry:

The thing about this birthday is that certain things I was sure would happen to me by now still haven't. I still have absolutely nothing. I could stuff tissues in a bra, but I'd feel so phony. Besides, I tried that. The tissues moved around and I ended up looking completely lopsided. And I don't have my period yet. Like a disgusting little girl. I know about a lot of stuff, some my mother wouldn't like me to know. Well, maybe she wouldn't mind my knowing as long as I don't do them. I think some of the girls in my class are crazy. Some have tried pot and one girl I know told me she went the whole way with a boy. Yuck. It gives me the creeps to think about that. Maybe when you get older it's different.

That reminds me. My mother has a new boyfriend. He doesn't stay over and I've never seen them kiss (my mother is so discreet!), but they sit close to each other in the living room and talk in low voices so I can't hear. He works for her magazine. Actually he's her boss. He's always trying to make me like him, patting me (ugh!) and complimenting me, telling me I'm going to be a beauty like Nora (my mother's name is Nora) when I grow up. I don't think he likes Sean much, though.

It's no wonder. Sean's a real mess these days. I think he does dope and he rides a motorcycle without a helmet. He's going to get himself killed someday—that's what my mother says. Once he ran away and stayed a week. We never found out where he went. Maybe that's why it's just as well that I'm not too grown-up yet—I don't want to be like Sean. I keep saying to myself that it's because Daddy left us, but I don't really think that's enough excuse. He left me, too, and I didn't turn into a mess. Anyway, Sean used to be nice to me, but now he's awful. He makes fun of me or ignores me. I think boys are terrible. Especially brothers.

That's enough for one day. I read this and it doesn't sound much like Anne Frank, but then my life is—thank goodness—different from hers. My English teacher says I'm a good speller and an exceptionally good writer for my age (that's what she said, "exceptionally good"), though. I guess that's from reading so much. I wonder if someday somebody will be reading this the way I read Anne's diary. She never thought anyone would read her most personal thoughts when she wrote them.

It amazed Meredith to think that just four days before she had been writing about things like her period and being a good speller. She felt she had been altered by a single day, by discovering about Lisa's death—her *murder*—and being interviewed by the police. And keeping Lisa's secret. It was as though an earthquake had come along, she decided, and shifted everything in her life to another place. She picked up her pen.

Monday, March 21

I didn't write over the weekend because my mother and Sean and I went up to Sonoma County, to the wine country, my mother calls it. We stayed at a darling bed and breakfast in Glen Ellen and visited Jack London Park and saw Wolf House, where Jack London never got to live, because it was burned down the night before he was going to move in. It looks like a regular ruin, with a whole bunch of chimneys—seven, I think.

I thought today I'd be writing all about the weekend. Instead, something awful has happened. Lisa was killed. It still sounds strange to say it—or think it or write it. I feel as though the phone's going to ring and it's going to be her saying we should go for a walk on Cliff Drive. All day in school, after we heard, I expected to see her coming out of class or walking ahead of me in the corridor. The principal got us all together in the auditorium and told us. Tomorrow instead of classes, we have to meet in groups with teachers to talk about it. It's supposed to be good for us or something. I won't be able to talk about it, I know I won't. I cried and cried when I heard, but somehow I don't feel it. I can't explain. It's as if I'm all hard inside. I wonder if everybody is this way when someone they love dies. It wasn't like this with Grandpa, though.

I don't know much about what happened. She was found in Richards West Park under some bushes, and she'd been there since Friday. I didn't even know she was missing, because we left right after school Friday. I think she was raped. I'm not sure what raped is, but I think it's when somebody forces you to go all the way. It makes me shiver to think of it.

The detective that asked me questions wanted to know about—better not say his name. (I can never be sure Sean

23

or Mother won't read this.) That was so dumb of me to mention him to the detective—he didn't have anything to do with this.

It's funny but I can't write anymore. I feel all chilly, as though I'm coming down with something. I think I'm going to take off my jeans and put on my warm quilted robe. I think Mother'll let me eat dinner in it tonight, because of what happened today.

Meredith sat a moment longer at her desk. She really did feel funny. After a while she got up, returned the journal to its hiding place and slowly began to change out of her jeans.

6

The Margolins knew nothing of a crush on an older man, and Jean was clear that her colleagues had expressed polite interest in the girls and no more. Meredith, she said, was given to fancy. As, she added sadly, Lisa had been.

Under protest, however, she gave them a list of family friends, male. As Pedersen had expected, it led to nothing. With the exception of one man, who was down with a bad case of the flu and whose wife had been with him all day Friday, the men had been at work, with witnesses to bear out the fact, and blameless. Interestingly, no one was offended by the request for this information. These were family men, concerned as to what they might do to better protect their own children.

Tate had located the boy in the math class, Jimmy Bush. He was tall for twelve, a shy, poetic-looking boy with large dark eyes, who seemed deeply embarrassed at the suggestion that Lisa had liked him. He saw her only in math class, he said, and couldn't even remember whether she'd been in school Friday. Tate noted his name and moved on.

It wasn't until Tuesday afternoon that Pedersen and Tate were able to interview the possible witnesses to the abduction of Lisa. The Water Exercise group that preceded the afternoon Youth Swim used no sign-up sheets. All members were known by appearance to the group leader and ritually paid their three dollars on entrance to the pool house. Some of the members were regulars; some came less often. These were the women who on Friday would have been leaving the pool just opposite the paths and woods at approximately the time of Lisa's death.

Pedersen waited until they had gathered for the Tuesday session, then he summoned them to the side of the pool. "Did any of you who was here Friday afternoon," he said, "see a young girl wearing a green jacket enter the wooded area across the road?"

"That's that dead girl, Lisa Margolin," one of the women commented.

"That's right. Anyone recall her?"

There was a long silence. After a while, one woman ducked a hasty glance at her companion. "You?" Pedersen asked.

"Well," said the woman, "I *think* I saw her. Remember, Edith?"

The other made a face intended to convey that she hadn't meant to become involved in this. "Yes, I guess so," she said reluctantly. "The one who was walking fast."

"Anyone else? We want to get this man before he does in someone else." Pedersen searched the faces around him. "Maybe one of your daughters." The face remained blank.

"It's terrible, a thing like that," one woman said. "To think there are people like that roaming around Bay Cove."

"It is terrible. That's why we need your help." But no more was forthcoming. Pedersen addressed the two women who thought they had seen Lisa. "Would you come with us for a minute?"

The women followed the detectives into the pool office. They were so clearly self-conscious about their half-clad state that Pedersen looked around and plucked a pair of towels from a stack. One draped the towel around her shoulders, the other laid it over her lap, skirtlike.

"Now," Pedersen said. "Tell me exactly what you saw."

Away from the group, they relaxed. "It was raining when we left. As we came out, I saw this young girl," said the first woman. "She had on jeans and a green jacket, and she was walking very fast down a path behind a man. I figured they were trying to get out of the rain."

"Behind him? Not with him?"

"No," said the other. "He was ahead. It was as though he was showing her the way."

"That's right," said the first. "As though they had to get someplace in a hurry and he was showing her the way."

"What did the man look like?" Tate asked.

"We didn't see his face—did you, Edith?" said the first woman.

"No. He was sort of"—Edith closed her eyes—"medium height, not tall. Dark hair, I think. Wearing—wearing—what was he wearing, Gerry?"

"I think a raincoat. I'm not sure. I think it was a tan raincoat."

"Yes," said Edith. "That was it, a tan raincoat. He was sort of stocky. And more like a boy."

"Than a man?" asked Tate.

"No," said Gerry, "he looked like a man. And not stocky. Just—regular. Not stocky."

"Do you think you'd recognize him again, from the rear, that is?"

The two women looked at each other. "No," said Edith. "You mean a lineup?"

"Yes."

"No. I'd never be able to recognize him, would you, Gerry? We weren't really paying attention. We didn't know she was going to be *murdered*."

Gerry shook her head sadly. "She's right. We're not much help, are we?"

"Yes, you've been helpful. I wish you could remember a bit more, but most people wouldn't have remembered this much. The man didn't turn or speak to the girl at all?"

"No. We didn't see his face. Really, you wouldn't even have thought they were together, except that they were both walking fast in the same direction, as though they had to get someplace in a hurry."

"Or out of the rain. We just saw them for a minute—they disappeared down a path toward the river almost as soon as we came out of the pool house," said Edith.

Pedersen nodded. "If you'll just give us your names and addresses, then. We probably won't need to bother you again, but just in case."

"I wish we—" said Edith, as she wrote down her name and address.

"You did just fine," Tate said. "Just fine."

After they had gone, he said, "Do you suppose he really did tell her there was an injured animal back there?"

"He told her something needed urgent action, that's for sure, though we may never know what. They weren't just getting out of the rain."

T here appeared to be no other sources. Even the groups of boys that usually played ball in the park had been discouraged by the onset of rain in the afternoon.

Except possibly for the objects found at the site of the killing, they had come to the end of their leads. The *Banner*'s request for information from anyone having seen a young girl in a green jacket in Richards West on Friday had brought no one forward. Pedersen rounded up the known sex offenders, asked them to wear raincoats to the lineup and presented them, rear view, to Edith and Gerry. Not only did that produce nothing, but the women were in stronger disagreement as to the man's appearance than before. Pedersen sighed and ushered them out.

The autopsy report cast no light; it was, in fact, odd. No tissue was found beneath the girl's nails, no foreign pubic hairs upon the body, no semen in or on her body. And, actually, she had not been raped. If there had been an attempt at penetration, apparently a struggle, followed by the strangling, had defeated that effort. Whether or not the man had had strangulation in mind was unclear. If Gerry and Edith's description had been correct, he had been undisguised; he may have considered murder a necessary act of self-protection. It was strange: no rape, the pulled-up jeans, the absence of fingerprints. Well, Pedersen reflected, the last wasn't strange. The steady rain had obliterated all fingerprints.

The objects they had found at the scene were not illuminating. A fragment of bamboo, tiny, cylindrical, hollow; it appeared to be part of a chopstick or some similar object. Lisa's mother didn't recognize it. A visit to the local Chinese restaurants turned up nothing. The others—a crushed Coke can and a wad of paper containing elementary school sums—as well as the piece of bamboo, could easily have been part of the debris that accumulates in parks. The items had been carefully bagged and labeled; Pedersen put consideration of them aside.

"What next? *Intermission?*" said Tate.

"I think so," said Pedersen. "Probably will get us nowhere, but there's always a possibility. Nothing else has been particularly enlightening."

They looked at each other. "No," said Ronald Tate. He shook his head.

7

Meredith slid her journal toward her on the desk and looked at it. She hated to write this, but how could anything be any worse than what she had written yesterday about Lisa's death? Besides, journals weren't only for writing *good* things; if that were so, Anne would never have written hers at all. Tonight Anne Frank's death and Lisa's death and even, somehow, her father's leaving them were all mixed up in her mind and in a way what she was going to write was like something dying, too. Slowly, she leaned forward and reached for her pen.

Tuesday, March 22 (after school)

I really don't want to write this. I just argued with myself about it but, as my mother always says, it's part of life and you have to accept it.

I wrote a letter to my father over a week ago. He hasn't called or come to see us in such a long time, I felt funny phoning, so I wrote the letter. I told him what I'd been doing in school and then said that Sean was upsetting Mother, and I thought maybe he was into dope. And that Sean and I were fighting an awful lot. And I said I missed him a lot.

I figured if I mailed it last Monday, he'd have it Tuesday—mail takes just a day—and he'd call or come over. I didn't hear a thing from him. No phone calls, nothing. I sort of offhand asked my mother if he'd called her, and she looked at me as if I was crazy and said, "Hardly. He's a bit preoccupied. Didn't you know?" Well, I gave up on hearing from him, although I felt just terrible all week, but then we went to Sonoma and I sort of cheered up and almost, well, I didn't forget about it, but I sort of pushed it way back in my head. Then Lisa was killed and I really forgot about it. It seems to me I can't stop crying, and Jennie's the same way. We talked in school today, and we both can't believe it. I keep expecting Lisa to call and read me a new poem she wrote. We're not the only ones, either. All the kids—well, all the girls at school were crying today, even the ones who didn't really know Lisa.

Anyway, I hadn't really thought about Daddy till today, when I got a letter from him. Not a phone call or a visit, but a letter. (I wonder if he knows Lisa was my best friend. I guess she wasn't when he was living with us.) I was let down, but at least it was something. I came in here to my room and I almost ripped it, I opened it so fast. Do you know what it was? It was typed by his secretary— there were those funny little initials to show someone else typed it. And it said—well, I'll copy it:

Dear Meredith,

Sorry I didn't get back to you sooner, but I've had a bitch of a week. (Shouldn't say that to you, should I?) I'm sorry you and Sean are battling, but it's all part of growing up. I'm sure, knowing you, that you're handling it. If I ever get out from under this mountain of work, I'll come by, but it looks as though it'll be a while.

31

Glad to hear everything's going well at school. Keep hitting those books.

Daddy

Not even a love. It sounds so—as though he isn't connected to me at all. It was the kind of letter he could have written anybody. *I cried after I read it. I guess I don't really have a father anymore.*

This has been the worst week of my life.

She sat looking at the letter from her father that she had just copied, the perfectly typed letter on his office stationery, with his secretary's initials. Then she rubbed her hand across her wet eyes, wadded the letter into a ball and threw it as hard as she could across the room.

8

Intermission's offices were above an import-export shop on the town's outdoor mall in a building that reminded Pedersen that Bay Cove had been around for a while. The front office, its link with the public, was reached by a steep, narrow staircase. It consisted of one square room. Along one side was a counter, behind which a harried-looking middle-aged woman worked at a desk. Beyond her, several tall steel file cabinets lined the wall. Opposite the counter stood a pair of unmatched and uncomfortable-looking straight-backed chairs.

"Welcoming," Tate murmured.

The woman finished the paragraph she was typing and gave her attention to the detectives. They identified themselves.

"Oh." The woman's face crumpled as though she were about to cry. "Mrs. Margolin's daughter."

"That's right. May we have a word with the managing editor?"

"Mr. Altman. Yes. I'll check and then I'll take you right through."

Kurt Altman's office was not much of an improvement over

the outer one—it was obvious the magazine operated on a shoestring—but it did cut him off from the activity and chatter of the others. He closed the door behind him.

"Jean isn't back at work yet, I'm sure you know. Jesus, what an awful thing that was. An only child, too. She must be desolated." He was a man who appeared to be in his late forties, with dark hair just touched by gray at the temples but otherwise youthful looking, almost boyish in his movements.

"She is. She has control of herself, but she's suffering. It's good that she works."

"I suppose. Actually, I told her she could take off any time she needs. Maybe I shouldn't have done that."

"I imagine it was comforting to her to know you all cared."

"Cared!" Kurt Altman stared at him. "I have two little girls!" Then, his face puzzled, as though he had just realized who the two men were, he said, "What can I do for you?"

"It's about that visit Lisa and her friend Meredith made to the magazine. It can't have been long ago."

"No. Two or three weeks ago. Actually, three. Why are you interested in that? You don't think—"

"We don't think anything. We'd just like to know who they met, how well acquainted they got. They may have said something—you know kids. Showing off—or just confiding."

Altman was quiet for a moment. "I can't believe—"

"This is pretty routine, Mr. Altman. We're checking everything in this girl's life in the past few weeks."

"Yes. Well. Let's see. Nora and Jean brought them in—actually, it was Nora's idea. Both the kids write, it seems. They checked it out with me, and I thought it was a fine idea. We don't go into the schools or anything of that sort, so I figured this would be our contribution to youth." He smiled. "I took them around to see people who represented different aspects of the operation. There was even a local filmmaker here—actually, Nora was planning to interview him, so the kids sat in on that and then later accompanied Nora and the photographer to his house for photographs. But first, let's see. They talked with our music editor, she's a woman. And our design man. We're working on a new format for the magazine, and he's been

34

hard at that. And I talked with them." He looked uneasily at Pedersen.

Pedersen waved a hand dismissively. "You really showed them the works."

"The editorial end, at least. Actually, we have twenty-three editors and contributors." He said it with some pride. "It was just a sampling."

"What is it that Jean Margolin does?"

"She covers local shows and exhibits; actually, we cover the whole county. She reviews art museum, gallery, and university shows and so on." He looked with some doubt at the detectives. "I'm sure you know the magazine."

Pedersen smiled. "We get *Intermission*."

Tate said, "Sometimes two copies." The magazine was distributed free, paid for by copious advertising.

"Too many people get two copies. If you'll stop by the desk outside, Mary can straighten that out. Now, you want to meet these people? Joel, that's the filmmaker, you'll have to see someplace else; he was just here for the interview. But I can introduce you to Robert and Shelley."

"First, what about you? Did Lisa say anything that would have led you to assume she was seeing a boy or man or was into anything she shouldn't have been?"

"Lord, no. Most of the time she sat there with her mouth shut. Actually"—he grinned—"with her mouth open, figuratively speaking. She was very interested. She did ask me if we published any poetry. I had to tell her no." He paused, as though remembering. "Poor kid. Guess she won't be writing any more poems."

"Nothing else?"

"No. Actually, she asked intelligent questions; they both did. Seemed to be a bright kid. I'd never met her before."

"All right. Let's try the others."

Robert Carter was poring over a sketch. He waved a hand as the men approached him. "I have it, Kurt," he said with pleasure. He was a dark-haired young man, surely not yet thirty, with intelligence and humor in his face.

Altman introduced the detectives. "Robert," he said to Ped-

35

ersen, "is our latest acquisition, and a welcome one. He's just back in Bay Cove after a try at the big world out there." He grinned. "I know all about that. I tried San Francisco and gave up on it and came home."

"You're native to Bay Cove, both of you? That's rare."

"Yes, it seems to be the town people come back to. Even Joel—he's the filmmaker I mentioned—gave up on Portland. When I heard that, I decided a return to Bay Cove must be a prerequisite for having anything to do with *Intermission*."

"And where were you?" Pedersen asked Robert Carter.

"New York, of course. It's *the* place for a designer, an artist of any kind, but I guess I'm spoiled. I missed Bay Cove, the accessibility—have you ever tried to get anywhere in New York? Buses that stop every two blocks and subways where you may be ripped off at any moment. And I missed the bay and the weather. I didn't like having to spend an hour and a half getting to the ocean. Or freezing to death in winter." He grimaced. "It's an exciting city but hell to live in."

"Then you're glad you're back?"

"Well, I'm not making what I was in New York, and I miss the excitement. My—accommodations at the moment aren't what they were, but on the whole I'm glad. Aren't you, Kurt?"

Altman nodded. "I like the scale of things here better. Robert, these detectives want to talk to us about the girls' visit—Nora and Jean's daughters."

"Yes? Was there something—"

"We wondered if you had talked with them to any extent, Mr. Carter."

"Let's go in my office," Kurt said. Several heads had turned toward them.

In the office, Pedersen said, "We're wondering if the kids said anything while they were here. When they're in a grown-up situation, kids sometimes like to boast a little, talk as though they're adults. Did either of them say anything about friendships with boys or men, anything like that?" Pedersen felt he was being vague. What am I here for? he wondered. Am I trying to get information or am I really just looking these men over?

"Lisa—the one who was . . . said she wrote poetry. She

showed me a poem she had in her pocket. About sitting on the rocks by the water and seeing the fog come in. Poetry isn't my forte, but it seemed pretty good to me."

"That's the sort of thing I mean," Pedersen said encouragingly.

Carter shook his head. "That was about all of that nature."

"Actually, I know Meredith a little," Kurt said. "I've dropped by her apartment and run into her. She never said anything in the least leading—mostly it's complaints against her brother."

"Yes?" Pedersen knew.

"He's eighteen and she thinks he's pretty strange. I suppose that's usual at that age."

"Strange in what way? Did she ever specify?"

"No. Look here, you're not—he's just a kid."

"Eighteen-year-olds have been known to commit crimes. Is he on drugs?"

Kurt Altman looked uncertain. "I have no idea. She—Meredith—accuses him of it, but I doubt that it's anything but pot. Say, I'm sorry I brought it up. The Cranes are friends of mine."

"You haven't told us anything we weren't aware of," Pedersen said. "We've met Sean. Remember, this is murder. You can't pussyfoot around pertinent information simply to spare someone's feelings. That's why I wanted to talk to you two and anyone else who met the girls."

"Oh, God," Kurt said. "I forgot somebody."

"Who's that?"

"Our ad man. We depend on advertising to keep the magazine afloat, and he could charm a bag lady into running an ad. Syd Pagano. The girls talked to him."

"Is he in today?"

"He's someplace around. Let me get him."

"So you're liking *Intermission* after the big city?" Tate said conversationally to Carter.

Robert Carter glanced toward the open door. "I could do with more money. It's a hell of a good little magazine, though, and it'll be a lot better when we finish the redesign job. Kurt's a good man to work with. Everybody likes him."

Kurt, as though responding to his name, appeared in the doorway. With him was a young man clearly of Mediterranean heritage—dark haired, dark eyed, with richly tawny skin. His face was sleekly sensuous, saturnine. This, Pedersen thought, may not be the one Lisa had the crush on, but it's hard to believe he got past the observant eyes of those two.

"Syd Pagano," said Kurt. "Advertising man par excellence."

Pagano laughed. "Kurt gets carried away." He leaned forward to shake Tate and Pedersen's hands. "I understand you're asking if we were told anything interesting by the girls who visited." He paused and shook his head. "Terrible thing. Jean must be a wreck. And her husband."

"Yes. Have you anything you can tell us about the girls? What did they talk about?"

"Not much. They both said they wrote. Lisa wrote poetry, the other kid said she wanted to be just like Anne Frank. They seemed poised kids, not too shy, as though they'd been around adults a lot. Lisa mentioned that she had written some poems about her dog. Brandy or some name like that. She seemed crazy about him."

"Oh, yes," Robert said. "She mentioned him to me, too. He was named Candy, I think."

"Were the girls—flirtatious with you?"

Pagano smiled. "They didn't come on to me. I guess I wasn't their type."

Kurt said, mildly shocked, "They're little girls."

"Not all that little. Pubescent girls are interested in the opposite sex," Pedersen said.

"But," Kurt insisted, "not in *men*. Boys, maybe."

"Maybe. Now this Joel—what's his last name and where do we find him? And I should talk to your music person, the woman."

"It's Joel Sterne with an *e* at the end. He's in the book. I'll get Shelley for you."

"Never mind. Just head us toward her. And thank you." He nodded to the others. "You've been helpful." As an afterthought, he asked, "You're both married?"

They stopped.

"No, I play the field myself," Syd Pagano said. A smile twisted his mouth, but his voice was unamused.

"I'm not currently married, either," Carter said coldly.

"That didn't go over very well," Tate remarked as they walked back to the music critic's desk.

"No." Pedersen grinned. "It didn't."

Shelley was a small slender woman who had an unanchored appearance, as though she might absently drift off into the air in midconversation. She was vague about the visit. When, finally, she recognized what it was the detectives wanted, her face brightened. "Oh, *yes*. They were so *enthusiastic*," she said. "They acted as though they wanted to move right in. And Lisa—to think she wasn't even going to *be* here three weeks later. It's awful."

"Did they say anything special to you, confide anything?"

"Well,"—she looked shyly from one to the other—"they talked about how handsome all the men, the editors and Syd, were. I see those men all the time, and to me they just look like—people, but the girls, especially Lisa, seemed very taken with them as romantic figures." She giggled and then put her hand over her mouth as though she had done something untoward. "It was rather *endearing*."

Leaving the building, Tate said, "Actually, they aren't bad looking, as a group." He laughed. "*Actually*. It's infectious."

Pedersen laughed. "Yes, I noticed. Nervous mannerism, probably."

"You think Altman was nervous? But they are a handsome bunch. That Pagano. And Carter. And I suppose Kurt Altman would be considered attractive if one were looking for a father figure. At that age, Lisa might have been."

"All dark haired. Interesting that two of them, at least two, knew about Lisa's dog and her affection for it."

"You really think that's how the murderer got to her?"

"I don't know. But it's a point, all the same."

"If they had used the dog, would they have mentioned him to us?"

"They—or he—might think we have no notion of a ruse involving an animal. For that matter, we don't have any idea

39

how she was lured into those woods. We're getting ahead of ourselves."

"It was also interesting that three of them had been living out of Bay Cove."

"You mean—"

"Yes. Big cities. Anonymity. Places where the murder of a child is more common."

"So if this weren't the first, we'd never know it. And there was nothing distinctive, no mark, nothing left on her body that we could use to check in another city. It's something to think about."

"You know," Tate said, "we're talking as if one of those guys is guilty. Probably none of them gave the kids another thought once they left."

Pedersen sighed. "Probably not."

They had called the filmmaker.

"Good day to come," he announced as he let them in. "I just cleaned house. When *Intermission* told me they'd want a picture here, I decided I'd better give the place a once-over. I liked it so much that way, I've been making a regular habit of it." He laughed.

Joel Sterne was not much over five eight and not good-looking in any usual sense. Heavy shoulders made him seem squat; he was black haired, weathered looking. In his deeply tanned face his eyes were startling, the whites very white, the irises so black they seemed one with the pupils, the eyes surrounded by laugh wrinkles. His was what one would call, at first glance, a likable face. Even his mustache was jaunty.

Pedersen and Tate were not concerned with likable faces. Pedersen asked his questions.

"I talked with Lisa and the other one—Meredith, wasn't it? Not much. Nora Crane was doing the interview, and then we came back here to photograph me in my natural habitat. The kids were excited over meeting a filmmaker—I didn't point out to them that they may never see the film. I haven't had any distribution to speak of. Not one commercial distributor has bitten." He shrugged. "Why discourage them at so young an age?"

"What is the film, Mr. Sterne?" Tate asked.

"It's called *Bible Story*, for reasons too complicated to go into now. The study of a young girl caught up in the drug world. I set up a little company with the goal of turning out low budget films, I mean really low budget. Our backers have shown a lot of confidence in *Bible Story*. They like its topicality, they feel it has aesthetic integrity. We even have a psychiatrist among our backers who says it has clinical validity. Go tell the distributors." He shook his head. "All we need is one—or maybe two—and we can't get one to touch it."

This must be his sales pitch, Pedersen thought. Maybe the man should move away from generalizations about the film's aesthetic properties to something more concrete, like how many teenagers will want to eat their popcorn watching it. Nonetheless, he was curious about the film.

"How'd you happen to choose your topic?" he asked.

"It interested me. I figured anything on drugs would go down today. And on teenagers. Three-quarters of the audience for films today are teenagers. Apparently I was wrong."

"Did Lisa and Meredith express interest in your subject?"

"Yes, but they were awed—it wouldn't do to put much stock in their reactions. Nice kids, those two. It's very sad what happened."

"Yes, it is. Did Lisa say anything while she was here that would give you an idea as to how she could have gotten into that situation?"

Sterne looked around the room as though the answer might be found there. It was a studio-living room. A huge worktable dominated, and in one corner, a double bed. For the rest, a clutter of large cushions with faded covers substituted for comfortable chairs. Four straight-backed chairs and shelves crammed with books constituted the remainder of the furnishings. The windows looked as though they had just been

41

washed; perhaps that was the housecleaning to which Sterne had referred.

"She didn't say much at all," Sterne said. "She talked about writing poetry, that was about it. She asked if I wrote any." He grinned. "I had to confess I'd tried poetry, and every piece I sent out had been firmly rejected. I know you want information on Lisa, but I'm not your man. I probably wouldn't have recognized her if I'd run into her afterwards, it was that brief a visit."

"Then I guess that's it," Pedersen said. "If there's a local showing of your film, let us know." He smiled. "And good luck. Maybe somebody will pick it up."

"Maybe it'll be a sleeper. All the reviewers will discover it," Tate added.

"It only should," Sterne said. "It only should."

9

Meredith turned on her bed lamp and reached for her robe, which lay across the foot of the bed. She fished her journal from beneath the mattress and padded barefoot to the desk. The house was silent; she supposed everyone was asleep. She picked up her black felt-tipped pen and began to write.

Tuesday, March 22 again (only it's midnight)

I couldn't sleep till I said FORGET IT! (Can you tell a diary to forget it?) I've decided I'm not going to be hurt and mad at Daddy's letter. He probably is having a "bitch" of a week. He works very hard. I remember how many nights he worked late when he lived with us (though my mother was always saying in that sarcastic voice she has sometimes, "Work again tonight, darling?"). But I think it was work, and he might really have been her darling if she'd been decent to him sometimes. Oh, I can't get into that. My mother says I don't understand what it's all about and she's right. I don't understand, any of it.

But the important thing is, he did write to me, even if his dumb old secretary typed the letter. He was probably embarrassed to say Love, at the end because he was dictating. I know he loves me, and Sean, too, only I wish he'd come around more and show it.

I just had to say this. I feel better now. I couldn't let my journal be spoiled because I'm acting like a baby.

10

It had been exactly a week since the wife of Kurt Altman, managing editor of *Intermission*, had decided her husband was unfaithful to her. On her way to run errands and pick up her younger child at day care, Libby Altman had veered off her usual route and cut around to see a wall of wisteria recently described in the *Banner* as the oldest and most lush in Bay Cove. It hung the length of the wall, almost the length of a city block, like fat clusters of pale purple grapes, at the peak of its fullness with barely a petal fallen to the ground. She caught her breath and slowed the car.

Still smiling, she had turned back by way of Ash Street when she saw her husband. Always when she ran into him unexpectedly, she felt a little lift of spirits; today was no different. She speeded up a bit and then eased back on the gas pedal. She was sure it was he, a man who even at a distance looked like Kurt, wearing a jacket like the one Kurt had worn that day, a man who moved like Kurt. Yet he was getting out of a parked car unfamiliar to her, and he and the woman who had been driving were walking up a path to enter an apartment house. Libby's fingers froze on the horn. Afterward she asked herself why she had not simply honked furiously.

None of the errands she had planned was crucially important; without thought, she slid her car alongside the curb and turned off the ignition, waiting for Kurt to come out. A half hour passed and still she sat on, growing increasingly uneasy. When he came out she would ask him what he was doing there. Who the woman was. After an hour, with the possibility of being late for Cory, she pulled out and drove away. What she wanted was not to go for Cory, but to lie down across the seat of the car, draw up her knees and become small.

Still, she could have been wrong. After close to a week, she was sure she was wrong; nonetheless, she had decided finally to say something to Kurt.

He had come home from work, his usual breezy manner in full force; for all his boyishness, he was a hearty man. She had to smile as he told her in detail a rambling tale of mislaid prints for a lead article in an issue momentarily about to go to press. She did love him; she really couldn't believe he was unfaithful. And yet, there was that other business lately. The sex.

It had always been Libby's impression that Kurt ran the magazine single-handed, he fussed so over decisions, the quality of photographic reproduction, the art work, even the ads. And she recognized his hand in many of the writings that were unattributed. But after seeing him enter the apartment house with the woman, she had checked the list of contributors and was amazed at their number: twenty-three, ten of them women. In the phone book, several of the women were listed with a phone number but no address. None claimed Ash Street.

She was not looking forward to the confrontation with Kurt. She had thrown a meal together—meat loaf, defrosted vegetables—and she was the one who was having trouble getting it down. She pushed her serving around her plate while the others, uncomplaining, wolfed their dinners quite as usual.

Kurt noticed. "Not feeling well?"

She forced a smile. "Just not hungry. I guess I'm tired. There's nothing but ice cream for dessert." Perversely, she wanted him to notice that she had been inattentive to the meal.

He nodded. "That's okay, we like ice cream. Don't we, muffin?" Kurt doted on the girls. He turned to Cory. "How about that, mouse?" He addressed them always as small animals or inanimate objects, as though he had forgotten their names, Katerine and Corinne, and was trying gracefully, to cope with the fact. Usually it amused Libby. Tonight it annoyed her.

As she bathed the girls and read their bedtime stories (*The Elephant's Child* again for Cory, the next chapter of *Charlotte's Web* for Kate), she reflected that it was just as well that she was going to speak to Kurt: the discomfort of the unspoken questions nudging away at her was beginning to make her irritable with him.

She sank onto the couch; she was tired. Anxiety was tiring. "Your pleasure tomorrow night." Kurt nodded agreeably. They took turns putting the children to bed; if it had been up to Kurt he would have been in charge every night and the two girls would have had ten o'clock bedtimes. He was an indulgent father. Actually, she thought with a welling of emotion, he was a good father. Perhaps if he were up to something, she'd be better off to look the other way, not say anything to him. Some wives did that. Husbands strayed, especially at Kurt's age, sometimes briefly, inconsequentially, and then returned to the fold. She knew as soon as she spoke the words of her suspicion their relationship would be altered irrevocably.

"Kurt," she said, but he broke in on her.

"A couple of detectives visited the magazine today."

"Detectives? What for?"

"You know that little girl who was found in the park? She and a friend of hers visited us—their mothers both work for the magazine. The police wanted to know if the kids had said anything, given a hint as to anything odd."

"That woman works on the magazine? You didn't say anything."

"I guess I didn't. She does gallery reviews. You've met her. Jean Margolin."

She rummaged up a dim memory of a small, thin, rather

pretty woman. "I guess so." Odd that Kurt hadn't talked to her about the murder. She herself would have been full of it, especially if it were someone she knew.

"I spoke to her this morning. She's pretty upset."

"I should think so! Were there other children?"

"No, apparently Lisa was an only child." He gave an impatient gesture. "Let's talk about something else."

"I was about to. Kurt—" She was a coward. "Kurt, what do you do every day?"

"What do I do?"

"Well, I mean do you stay there at the magazine all day?"

"Usually. Why?"

"I just wondered. Do you ever have to go out to see writers? Or artists?"

"What? What's roused all this sudden interest?"

"Well, do you?"

"Usually not. They come to us. What are you getting at, Libby? Do you think I'm not earning my keep at the magazine, I'm goldbricking?"

"No." His old-fashioned phrases kept her aware of the difference in their ages. Her mother had been sure the eighteen years between them would be unbridgeable. Right now, she would be saying I told you so.

"No, I don't think you're goldbricking. I just realized I have no idea where you are all day. What you do. The other day I called around three and you weren't there."

He met her gaze impassively. "I must have stepped out for a minute. Did you leave a message? No one told me you called."

"No, I didn't. I tried again later, but you were still out."

"Who'd you speak to? They know where I am when I'm away from my desk." Then it occurred to him. "What were you calling about, anyway?"

"Nothing important; I can't even remember. But it made me realize I have no idea what you do when you leave the house in the morning."

He laughed. "Believe me, what I do is put my nose to the grindstone. Next time leave a message." He picked up the newspaper.

She hesitated. "I even thought I saw you one day—over on Ash Street. I guess if you were at the magazine all day, it was someone else."

He was reading. "Must have been," he said.

She sat staring at him. Could it have been someone else? She was close enough to see that he had on his gray jacket. Hadn't he? He didn't seem in the least like a guilty husband hiding something. She stood up and went over to kiss the top of his head. He looked up, surprised, then affectionate. "I'm just an old man," he said, grinning up at her. "Sitting here with my paper when there's a gorgeous creature like you around."

She smiled, too, suddenly relieved. "Oh, I wouldn't say an old man." But—was that, maybe, the problem with the sex lately?

11

On Thursday Meredith woke early. The house was still, everyone asleep. Yawning, she slid from under the covers, moved her bare toes over the cold wood of the floor till she found her slippers, and stood up and reached for her quilted robe. She liked the robe; it filled her out a little, made her look like less of a string bean. The top was puffy, which created the impression that she had something there. She sighed. She supposed she'd be like her mother; she wasn't exactly bosomy, either. She hoped not.

Turning to look at her silhouette in the pink-sprigged robe, she considered going out to the kitchen for some breakfast and then decided it could wait. This was a good time to write in her diary, when the house was quiet and her mother wasn't around thinking up something for her to do. Or Sean coming into her room, being weird. Most weekdays she couldn't write in the morning, things were so hectic getting ready for school.

She opened her red-bound journal.

Thursday, March 24

Jennie didn't feel well yesterday and she skipped ballet and came over. We sat in my room and talked and talked. We kept remembering things Lisa said or did and a couple of times we had to laugh, but we were crying, too, all the time. I don't feel so hard inside anymore.

On top of everything else, I had a fight with my mother. I can't even remember what over. Oh, I remember what started it. She said I acted as though I had no responsibilities around the house. It seems to me I do plenty around here. Every time she works late, I fix Sean's and my dinner, and every Saturday I put the laundry through, and I do my own ironing. I hardly have any time to see my friends at all. Sean doesn't do anything. He never even remembers to take out the garbage.

But the fight sort of got bigger and bigger, and pretty soon we were both yelling, with Sean sitting there with a sneer on his face, smoking a cigarette. (She hates him to smoke. That's why he does it.)

Anne didn't get along with her mother, either, but she had a father, which made a lot of difference. I don't even see mine anymore. These men my mother brings home give me the creeps. Lately there's been only the one, and he doesn't keep closing the door the way the last one did. (What did he think I thought? I knew what they were doing, even if they thought they were being so clever.)

Once my mother said to me that she's lonely and she needs what she calls male companionship. I told her it was her own fault she's lonely and she began to cry, and then I felt bad. But she was awful to my father, so naturally he left. She's always saying what Sean needs is a father—why didn't she think of that before she drove him away? But I must admit Sean needs something. He's getting to be a worse and worse mess.

This new boyfriend's name is Kurt, with a K he told me, as if I was going to write it or something. (Of course, Mother says he's just a friend, but that's what she always says. The whole business of her men depresses me.) Anyway, I didn't like him at first. My mother says I take what she calls an irrational dislike to people. Maybe I do. Maybe I just don't like any of her boyfriends. Maybe I'd like my own father back .

Anyway, we went to the magazine. I never thought of my mother as a writer before (dumb of me, she does work for a magazine), but I realized she's just like me. She likes to write! She does all the movie reviews and gets to see practically every movie there is (I did know that). She had some corrections to do, so Kurt came in and took us around and introduced us to people. And I liked Kurt. It's the first time. He introduced us to them as if we were adults, too. I liked that.

And Kurt must have realized I wasn't acting the same, because when we left, he said to my mother, "Your daughter and I have made friends." He meant us, not the people he introduced us to. And it was true, too. This is the first one of my mother's boyfriends I've really liked.

Anne called her diary Kitty. I wonder if I'd write better if I gave mine a name. I have friends and I don't live in an attic like Anne, so maybe it would be a little funny for me to do that, but I can see that writing to somebody makes it seem more like a real conversation. The most important thing to me, though, is to be honest. I'll bet people write diaries thinking about somebody someday finding them, and then they put in a whole lot of stuff to impress people. It's hard to be honest, but if you aren't, what's the use of a diary? You can't tell people some of the thoughts you have, even Jennie I can't tell, and she's my best friend next to Lisa. (I don't want to think about that any more now.) But a journal you can tell. And someday when I'm old, maybe I'll read what I wrote and know what I was like when I was twelve.

Twelve is an awful age, really. It's not—I don't know, it's not teens and it's not being a little girl, it's sort of in between. When I'm a teenager, I'll be able to do all sorts of things, or so my mother says. (She keeps moving the date *ahead, though—I suppose when I'm a teenager, she'll think of some other age for me to do things.) I think she's afraid I'll turn out like Sean. Yuck! I wouldn't be like him no matter what age I was.*

I hear my mother out in the kitchen. I'm getting sort of hungry. I guess I'll go out there. And probably fight with her again. I hope she's in a better mood than last night. I think what started her up was that phone call she got after dinner, probably from her boyfriend. I think he must have been telling her he couldn't come over and it made her mad. Angry, I mean. I wish I could remember to write the way Anne does.

Meredith rose from her desk and slid the book into its mattress hiding place. She was surprised she felt so good this morning, after crying all afternoon and then ending up in a fight with her mother. But she did feel good. Maybe it was because she had decided her father loved her, after all.

She combed her hair so her mother wouldn't send her back to do it and opened the door of the bedroom. She could smell bacon frying; her mother must be trying to make things up to her. Usually her mother didn't serve bacon, she said she'd discovered it was full of nitrites, and Meredith missed the time when her mother hadn't known that. Suddenly she was ravenous. Mothers were good for something.

12

"Carl," Freda said, "do you realize you've been sitting there playing with those beads for almost fifteen minutes?" They were having drinks before dinner, an evening ritual, Pedersen with his feet on the hassock of his favorite chair, Freda curled into a corner of the couch. "You haven't said one word to me."

Carl Pedersen glanced down at his hand, which held the green jade worry beads he had bought when he and Freda visited Greece. He was unaware that he rolled them back and forth between his fingers as he sat sipping his vermouth.

He slipped them into his pocket. "It's this damned case," he said. "I can't get it out of my mind."

"The little girl?"

"Yes. Lisa Margolin. I got such a *sense* of her from her family. And from her poem." He shook his head.

"Her poem?"

"Yes, a haiku, Ron said it was. Want to hear it?"

"You memorized it?"

He nodded. "It's short." He repeated it to her. "It struck me that it wasn't the sort of poem just any kid would write. And her friend, she seems exceptional, too." He looked across the room at his wife. The late afternoon light warmed her skin. In another half hour, dusk would darken the room. It was a room he loved to come home to. Uxorious, his wife teased him. And home-loving. It was true. "No TV that I could see, in either house," he said.

"That must have pleased you." Although he himself watched television occasionally, Pedersen's thoughts on the subject of children's viewing were violent, as violent as the shows television offered. "Let's hear that poem again."

He repeated it.

"You know, that's really very nice. She must have been a bright little girl."

"Apparently she was. Bright, disciplined, thoughtful. You should have seen her room." He sighed. "Just not bright enough."

"She was a child, Carl. Just a kid."

"I know. All id. Imagine when you're twelve the pleasure of having an adult interested in you. The romantic possibilities. And keeping a secret from your parents. She didn't sound like a particularly rebellious kid, but still—brightness has nothing to do with it. Reason goes by the board. It's been demonstrated over and over."

"I know. Remember when Carrie—"

Pedersen raised his hand. "Don't. I don't think I can listen."

"Come on, Carl, I didn't mean—Carrie never went with strange men."

"No, but you're suggesting that she could have."

"That's not so. Not Carrie. She'd never have done that."

He looked at her. "That's exactly what Lisa Margolin's parents are saying right now, you can be sure of it. Exactly what they're saying."

They were silent. Freda reached for her husband's hand.

After a moment Pedersen withdrew his hand. "Her friend said she'd have gone with anyone who said an animal was in danger. But that means the guy had to know that about her. The problem is, Freda, we've reached a sort of dead end. Two women saw her at a distance hurrying along a path after a man, but it could have been any male—a teenager, someone mature, anyone. The women had no real fix on him; they weren't even sure of his size and shape. None of the family friends seemed to qualify. Her classmates are too young."

"What do you do in a case like that?"

"You put it in an open file," he said bitterly. "No, we'll keep on it, but—you don't want to know."

"I can guess." She hugged herself. "You wait."

"Yes. And with no idea where or when he'll move again. Or even if. I've never had a case quite like this."

"They're common enough. You've just managed to avoid cases involving kids."

"I know." He looked across at her, at her small, supple body, the cap of dark hair brushed softly around her face, and thought, God, she could be taken for a teenager. If you came upon her and didn't look too closely, she could. "Harbison insisted that I take this one. He was furious. I've never seen him like that." He grinned, putting out of his head notions that Freda might be mistaken for a child. "He even said *fuck*— Harbison! First time I've ever heard him even swear."

"He has a youngster," Freda said.

"That's it. I'm glad our kids are grown."

"Me, too." She smiled. "For several reasons. But I feel as though we've—what's the word, traversed, I guess—a—"

"Rocky terrain."

She laughed. "That thought *was* a little clichéd. But it's true. We got through without either of them taking drugs. Carrie didn't get pregnant till she was married and ready for a child. Matt's doing fine in school."

"*Now*. You've forgotten the running away."

Her smile faded. "Yes. I do tend to forget that whenever I can. So. You just have to wait till this—maniac does something else? What makes you think you'll catch him then?"

"I don't think that. I just hope maybe next time people will be alerted and lead us to him, that he'll get caught *before* he does anything. God, this is a terrible conversation, anticipating rape

56

and maybe murder." He stood up. "Let's change the subject. I'm going to get some peanuts."

She held out her glass. "Why don't you freshen our drinks while you're out there? Dinner won't be ready for another twenty minutes."

He brought her refilled glass without offering the bowl of peanuts. Freda did not eat peanuts. He returned to his chair.

"What is a pedophile, exactly, Carl? Isn't that what you call someone who preys on twelve-year-olds?"

"Someone who preys on young-looking ones, at least. You mean what's the clinical definition?"

She nodded.

"I once read a definition of pedophilia as the perversion of weak and impotent persons."

"But they *rape;* they can't be impotent."

"I don't think that literally means impotent. Maybe they're impotent in normal sexual relations. They're anxious with women their own age, I gather, so they choose less— threatening females for their advances. True pedophiles, that is."

"But I thought a lot of pedophiles were married men."

"They are. It's complicated, I'm sure, and I'm no psychologist. And who knows what sorts of relations they have with their wives? I'm inclined to think all sociopaths are a blend of things, but I haven't really looked into pedophilia much. I just know there are teenagers who go after little girls and that there are grown men, married or otherwise. It'd make it a hell of a lot easier if there were some simple formula."

"They go after boys, too."

"Yes, but the dynamics of that must be different." After a minute he said, "You know, we ran checks on all those men at *Intermission,* the ones who had met the girls."

"Did you find out anything?"

"Not a thing. Not so much as a speeding ticket. I think we must be off on that. And yet—"

"What about the brother? The friend's brother?"

"Never been picked up. He may be on drugs, though. You know what crack does—it makes you crazy. You know," he went on, "there was something someone said, someone at that magazine—"

"What was it?"

"That's the trouble, it slipped past me. I keep trying to remember. It'll come to me."

He reached for a peanut, broke it in half and checked for the dwarf as his father and he had done when he was a boy. It always comforted him to find the dwarf; in some way it was a reaffirmation of his father's honesty. And goodness. Every once in a while he acutely missed his father. Today had been such a day. He sighed, popped the peanut into his mouth and reached into his pocket to be sure the worry beads were there.

13

Libby introduced her friend Ruth Parmalee and Joel Sterne at a dinner party. Like most of Ruth's married friends, Libby considered her a responsibility; help Ruth find a man seemed to be the directive. After her husband's sudden and entirely unanticipated death, Ruth had not wanted another man, not for a long time. She had still been in love with her husband, had barely had time to get over being in that delicious first stage of love, when he had his fall. A fall. It seemed to Libby such a ludicrous end. Running down a flight of hospital stairs—he was still a resident—he had slipped, and the blow as he hit the hard stone steps had caused his brain to hemorrhage. He had never recovered consciousness; Ruth had never said good-bye to him. Libby shivered as Ruth recounted the cold that enfolded her when they called from the hospital, the sense of the bottom having fallen out of her life. Ruth's daughter had been just five.

Somehow, though, Ruth had come through it. Libby knew Ruth's husband had had insurance, although Ruth said they'd argued over his getting it, she being sure it was something that

could wait; and with her job and the social security payments for her daughter, she managed. Actually, she had been working even when he died, helping with finances until he was making more. The plan was that once he was really earning, she would return to school herself. That, of course, never came to pass. She was lucky to have the job working in Bay Cove's Department of Parks and Recreation. She'd been lucky she had some secretarial skills. Lately of course she had expanded those skills; by now she supervised five people and was a whiz on any computer. But then, she said cynically to Libby, who wasn't a whiz on a computer these days?

Joel had come on the scene a year before, when Libby and Kurt had all but given up on Ruth. Kurt had run into him somewhere, had heard he was a filmmaker and interesting, and had brought him home.

Libby seized on him and gave Ruth a big buildup. "He's just moved to town, he's good-looking, he isn't gay, he makes a living, he has no mother in evidence. He's around your age. What more could you want?"

"What more could *he* want? Old Hips Parmalee."

Libby was disgusted. "You talk about yourself that way, but you know perfectly well that you have one of those figures sculptors drool over."

"Henry Moore?"

Libby laughed. "No, you know—that one our mothers liked, I think he was big in the thirties or forties. Zorach, wasn't that his name? William Zorach?"

"Never heard of him. My mother wasn't into art."

"The main thing is that you know that's not a healthy attitude you have. You're only forty-two, and despite what you say about yourself and your figure, you look about thirty-five. You need a sex life. A love life. Somebody to care about, now that Barbara's grown and off to college."

"End of sermon?" Ruth looked at her friend. "Okay, okay, I'll meet the guy. Just don't expect big things. Really don't, Lib."

But Libby could see that Ruth was surprised. Joel wasn't good-looking, not in any usual sense, but he had a lot of laugh wrinkles, his eyes were startling, he was warm, comfortable,

60

the sort of person a woman felt even after a few hours that she'd known forever. Ruth and he began to spend time together.

One thing Ruth admitted she liked about him was that he didn't make demands. For a long time after her husband's death, Ruth had held back sexually; in her few brief affairs, she had always found it difficult to move into the intimacy she associated with her husband. Joel had gone along with her hesitation, hadn't pushed. Then, she confessed to Libby, one night after several glasses of wine, she had walked to where he stood at the other end of the room and said, "Let's," and taken his hand and led him into the bedroom. Since then it had been fine. But Joel didn't press for marriage, never asked her to commit herself to living with him. Libby wondered if someday Ruth would say "Let's" to him about that. And what his reply would be.

Ruth and Joel spent weekends together. Even if they didn't go out, simply stayed at her place or his, they reserved weekends for themselves. It was rare that Joel suggested that they get together in midweek.

This night he had.

He phoned shortly before dinner. Later, Ruth told Libby about the evening. About parts of it.

"Hi, what're you doing?" he had asked.

"Well," she said, "to tell the truth I was trying to decide whether to wash my hair or skip it till tomorrow."

"Skip it till tomorrow. How about if I come by and we go down to Simply Simpson Street for a drink? That appeal to you more than washing your hair?"

"You know, it does." They both loved country music. On Friday nights the place was jumping; they'd never been there on a weeknight. Tonight they might even be able to hear the singers.

"Good. I'll be there in twenty minutes."

Over a beer, she told him. "Libby saw Kurt going into some apartment house with a woman. He stayed for hours. She hasn't told anybody but me, but last night she was going to say something to him." She paused. "She's really upset. She doesn't know what to think."

"Probably something perfectly innocent."

"A likely story. You men do stick together."

"It's not that. There are a dozen possibilities that don't involve bed."

"Yes? Name three."

He had trouble. "Well, maybe he was doing magazine business. Maybe she's a single woman who had a problem—plumbing or something, and he went by to help."

"That's only two. And I don't think Kurt does plumbing."

He laughed. "There are sometimes surprising explanations for things people assume mean something else."

"They'd surprise me, that's certain. Kurt's too old for Libby, anyway."

"Maybe that's what she needs. Not like you. You need younger men." He was four years her junior. "Virile younger men."

"According to Libby, Kurt is virile."

He signaled the waiter for another beer. The roar of voices and laughter made it hard to hear or talk. Simply Simpson Street had turned out to be noisy even on weekdays.

"Although lately—" She paused. "I guess I shouldn't tell all this."

"I'm like a tomb. Tell me."

"Well, he hasn't been paying much attention to Libby—Kurt hasn't. Sexually. Not for over a month."

"God, you women really discuss the details, don't you?"

"Well, it made her suspicious. If a man suddenly loses interest in you sexually . . ."

"Sometimes it horrifies me to think what women expect of men."

"What do you mean? If Kurt normally—"

"It's not this about Kurt. But performance is the name of the game. A woman can have a headache or be tired or just not feel like sex, but a man is expected to be available and arousable at all times. Maybe I mean aroused."

"I don't think that. You're never too tired, but if you were—"

"You'd put it down to loss of interest in you. You'd start a fight about how sexually undesirable you are."

Ruth was indignant. "I would not."

"Maybe not you, but the average woman. I know."

"Nice to know I'm not the average woman." She ran her finger over the wet surface of her beer mug.

"You're not. You're very special." He looked at her affectionately. "I'm glad I came back from Oregon last year. I might not have met you."

"How come you called me tonight? This isn't one of our usual nights."

"I don't know. I just felt like it." After a pause he said, "I was visited by some cops yesterday."

"You were? What about?"

"About that little girl who was found Monday."

Ruth leaned forward. "You knew her?"

"No, no. She and another kid came by my place a few weeks ago. Their mothers work for *Intermission*, and I was being interviewed by one of the mothers. The kids sat in on the interview and then came to my place with her and the photographer. The police thought they might have said something."

"Did they?"

"No. But it made me a little uneasy having the police come, even if I didn't have anything to tell them."

She picked up her mug. "I should think it would. The whole thing gives me the creeps. Let's talk about something else."

On the way home, he said, "Do you . . . feel at all for the man who did it?"

"Who killed that little girl? God, no, he's a monster."

"He's not a monster, he's sick. He's driven by something he can't control. You don't think he *wants* to go around killing children?"

For some reason, his rational tone infuriated her. "That's like saying people who hack up their wives had unhappy childhoods. Or people who commit mass murders were abused as kids."

"They probably did. And were. Seventy percent of the men in prison were abused as kids."

"Does that excuse them?" She was a little startled at the rage she felt.

"It doesn't *excuse* them, it *explains* them." His tone was that of a patient adult with an emotional child.

"I don't give a fuck about explaining them!"

"All right. Calm down." He attempted to lay a hand on her knee.

She brushed if off. "How a man of your supposed intelligence—"

"Please, Ruth, don't start with the judgments about my intelligence. Besides intelligence has nothing to do with it, information does. If you prefer to remain so emotional you can't see the facts, there's nothing anyone can do about it."

Suddenly she felt she hated him. "And you *feel* for that man? He has your sympathy?"

"He's in the grip of some sort of obsession. And then he has to live with himself afterwards. And still have the same impulses that drove him in the beginning."

"Joel, your compassion extends beyond anything believable. Besides, for all we know, he gets his kicks from strangling kids. Pedophiles don't have one scrap of my sympathy."

He was quiet for a minute. Then he said, "They have mine."

"Can you imagine?" Ruth asked Libby later. "Sympathy? For a creature who'd do a thing like that? To Kate or Cory. Or to my Barbara. For a minute there, I really hated him."

Libby looked at her thoughtfully. "But you made it up?"

Ruth shrugged. "Yes, after a while. But *really* . . ." She could talk no more about it.

14

Pedersen, who had been interviewing Lisa's classmates, Lisa's teachers, even Lisa's pediatrician, since she had not yet visited any other doctor, was getting nowhere. The teachers knew Lisa as a quiet, industrious student. One, her English teacher, commented on her growing talent as a poet. All seemed to admire and like her, but they could supply no information as to how she occupied her time away from school. Her classmates were even less forthcoming. She had been a shy girl without a wide circle of acquaintances. Only Jennifer and Meredith really knew her.

The pediatrician's name was, aptly, Dr. Little. He was a big, warm-faced man with a thick mat of sand-colored hair and extraordinarily large hands; Pedersen could imagine him balancing a fat baby on one palm and grinning down at it. When Lisa had been a fat baby (or perhaps a slim one), Pedersen was sure Little had known every detail of her history. Now that she was—or had been—twelve, Little was less sure.

"Lisa Margolin. The name is familiar. I'll check."

"It may be familiar because it's been in the newspapers this past week," Pedersen said.

Dr. Little looked up from the file cabinet from which he had just drawn a folder. "You don't mean that little girl who was killed was one of mine?" Standing at the file cabinet, he opened the folder. "Here we are. Of course, *Lisa.* I haven't seen her in several years. Of *course*, Lisa." From his reaction, it would have seemed he had had no other patient by that name. "A very grown-up little girl. Even, I remember now, a very mature small child. Solemn." He scanned the slim folder. "Inoculations. Checkups. A visit a little over three years ago, when she had a prolonged bout with the flu. That's the last I have on her. Tell me, what happened?"

"I'm afraid everything we know was right there in the *Banner.* That's why I'm here. We're trying to pick up anything we can that might lead us to her killer."

Dr. Little shook his head, causing a lock of sandy hair to fall across his forehead. "I can't tell you anything. Perhaps her mother took her to someone else. Now that she's older, you know."

"She says not. She says Lisa has been in good health, and she saw no reason to take her to anyone. I was just grasping at straws, coming here."

The physician nodded. "That murder—you don't expect something like that in Bay Cove. This town's changing."

Pedersen got up to go. "That may be, but you'll find it can happen anywhere." He stopped at the door. "Today you find it anywhere. Thank you for your time, Doctor."

The visit had led nowhere, just as had the several hours the afternoon before when, with Tate, he pored over Lisa's poetry, borrowed from her parents. For the most part the poems concerned the sea, the sky, the sun, trees, the out-of-doors. Despite her anthropomorphizing of those inanimate things, she seldom drew on actual human beings as her subject. A single rather sentimental sonnet addressed to her parents on their anniversary departed from her pattern. Several haikus were addressed to or were about her dog, Taffy. The affection expressed in them confirmed her friend Jennifer's surmise that

66

an abuductor could have lured her with the story of a hurt animal.

A single poem was the exception; they read it with interest.

> Seated on a rock,
>> blue-clad knees, bare feet, he listened.
> She talked of poetry.

"Do you suppose that's the guy? She knew him?" said Tate.

"Could be. Sounds like someone she met down at the water, not the park."

"He could have taken her to the park."

"Yes, he could. Sounds like a kid, rather than a man, doesn't it?"

"The jeans? Everybody in Bay Cove wears jeans. Even you wear them when you're off."

"Even me?" Pedersen smiled. "He listened to her talk about poetry; that was the way to get to her, all right." He turned over the scrap of paper. "I wonder when she wrote this. Her mother says she never dated anything."

"The paper looks fresh. She was a regular Emily Dickinson, all these bits of paper with poems on them. I don't see that this gets us anywhere, though, except that it suggests that she may have known the guy."

Pedersen grunted. It was true; they were making no head-way. Patrols checked Richards West Park with regularity, but nothing untoward had been observed, no older men with young girls, with one notable exception, which had resulted in an extremely embarrassed patrol officer who had politely stopped a couple that proved to be father and daughter and met the officer's inquiry with indignation.

It was depressing.

15

Meredith turned on her desk lamp. Her mother had a guest—Kurt—and Sean had gone out, God knows where, his mother shouting after him that it was pouring and to wear his raincoat. When Meredith read in the *Banner* about crack houses in town, she always envisioned Sean standing at a door on a dark side street, answering, "Buyer." The newspaper story had said they asked "Buyer or seller?" before they let anyone in. She was pretty sure he wasn't a seller. Yet.

Of course she didn't *know* that he did crack, it was just that it seemed to be the drug high school students used these days. She wondered if her mother knew. Or guessed.

She took out the journal and seated herself. The desk lamp cast a pool of light on the binding that made it seem to catch fire. She admired for a moment and then picked up her pen and opened the book.

Monday, March 28

I haven't written for a couple of days because I've been—well, it's a sort of long story and I'd better begin at the beginning.

Friday morning I woke up in agony. That sounds melodramatic, but it's true. I had these terrible cramps, like something pushing down inside of me. I could hardly move. I yelled for my mother, but she was in the bathroom getting ready for work and didn't hear me, so I crawled out of bed, really crawled. When I looked down I saw what the trouble was. I HAD MY PERIOD!

I would have been really happy—I've been waiting for about a year, it seems like, for this to start—but I hurt so much I couldn't be. I got to the bathroom and knocked on the door and called, and I guess my voice told my mother something was wrong. She was wonderful. She helped me get cleaned up—yikes, I am being honest in this diary, but Anne was, too. Anne even talked about what happened when they couldn't use the W.C. and had to use a preserving jar for what she called nature's offerings, so I guess I can talk about this. Then we went back to my room and I got into a fresh nightgown. I sat in a chair (huddled in a chair) while my mother changed the bed (she put on the company sheets, the ones with the yellow flowers) and then she sort of tucked me in. She brought me a couple of aspirins (they didn't do a thing) and a cup of tea. I always get tea when I'm sick, and something my mother calls milk toast, which nobody I know has ever heard of. The rest of the time we all forget tea and milk toast exist.

All the babying helped, and before Mother went to work, she called school to say I was ill. She was worried about leaving me, but she had to go, and I said I'd just curl up and sleep, if I could. She said she'd come home at lunchtime.

If having a baby is like that, I don't ever want one. My mother says I need to relax, menstruation is normal and stuff like that, but once that strange pushing down began

69

in my middle—really lower than my middle—I couldn't possible relax. And it went on for two days. Then all weekend I felt so tired I just lay around and read. That's why I haven't written. I know now that I'm capable of having a baby (if I lived in India or someplace where women have them at twelve), but I don't like it. Didn't like it. I'm all right now.

But something good came out of it. This morning I woke up feeling pretty good. Still little twinges, but nothing terrible. Mother came in and sat on the bed. "Meredith, I don't want you to go in to school this morning," she said. "I've made an appointment with my doctor for you." (I'm really writing like Anne. She told exactly what people said. It makes me feel like a real writer.) Then she went on, "I want you to shower and dress and come down to the magazine with me. I have a couple of things I have to do, and then we'll go see the doctor." She said I shouldn't have that much pain and that the doctor might know something to do.

So I put on a skirt and sweater—I don't know when I've had a skirt on—and got ready. I love going to the magazine. All those neat people and Kurt being nice to me. And Joel was there—I'm not sure what for—so I saw him again. And Robert. And Syd. I really call those people by their first names, just the way my mother does. It was worth being so uncomfortable just to have a chance to go to the magazine again.

The only thing was that going to the magazine reminded me of Lisa. Friday when I felt so awful I cried a lot about Lisa. I still can't seem to believe I won't see her again.

The doctor didn't say anything very meaningful. (My mother hates that word meaningful; she says it's meaningless.) He said he thought I might be anemic, and he had his lab assistant take a blood sample (she couldn't find my vein and just about killed me) and he said maybe I'd have to take iron. He gave my mother some pills that he says work better than aspirin (a sample he had in his office) and he told me to take it easy. Also he did an examination.

I won't talk about that. It was the most embarrassing thing I ever had to have, with my feet in stirrups—ugh!

Then when I got home something sort of strange happened. I was lying on my bed reading, when Sean came in (without knocking) and sat down beside me. He sat and stared at me till I began to get goose bumps. Then he said, "Well, Sis, I hear you've become a woman." I suppose with my staying home from school, my mother told him. She doesn't know how peculiar he is or she wouldn't tell him anything.

I looked at him and said, "So what? It's none of your business." Then his eyes went to where my breasts would be if I had anything, and he stared as if he could see right through my clothes, with a sort of sneer on his face, and said, "Not a real woman yet, though. Nobody's going to rape you," and got up and went out. I yelled after him, "You know, you're a real pervert!" Mother was in the other room, but she never said anything, so I guess she didn't hear what I yelled.

But I thought about what he said about my not being raped. Actually, everybody always says—said—that Lisa and I looked alike, and she wasn't developed, either, as flat as I am. I don't think the person who killed Lisa was looking for a "real woman." The whole thing gave me the shivers.

I'm beginning to feel tired again. I go back to school tomorrow. I missed a test and I have to make it up, so I'd better study a little now. Then I think I'll go to bed. Good night, Dairy. (That was silly. Anne never said anything like that. I must be beginning to grow up, I can see the silly things I do. Only not till afterwards.)

She closed the book and sat at her desk, looking at her science textbook. Really she felt very tired, but if she didn't study she wouldn't pass the test, and then she and her mother would have another fight. It was peaceful being on good terms with her mother and liking Kurt. She thought she'd like to keep it that way for as long as possible. She sighed and reached for the textbook.

16

Libby seldom dropped in on anyone. Her doing so this afternoon was motivated by a desire to talk to her mother straightforwardly, without prearrangement, preparation, prethought. Her mother had a way of thinking things through in advance, making up her mind and then paying no attention to anything that was said that did not concur with her conclusion. Libby wanted none of that today. She wanted to talk with her mother about the incident of Kurt and the woman.

The mobile-home park in which her mother lived was situated on a small lake, not much more than a pond, amidst tall, ragged eucalyptus trees that shed leaves over the houses and pocket-sized lawns. It offered variety within uniformity, single and double units painted variously and angled differently along the curving paths. The gardens were determinedly individual and carefully kept. Her mother's unit was painted a pale lemon color; the one next door into which a new neighbor had just moved (she had met him loaded down with boxes the time before when she visited) was white with black trim. The units complemented each other handsomely.

She found her mother at home. What she hadn't bargained for was her mother's having a visitor. For a moment she couldn't place the attractive young man sitting in her mother's living room having tea, then she remembered: the new neighbor—what was his name, Robert?

"Oh," she said, "you two have become friends." She turned to her mother. "We introduced ourselves the other day, Robert and I. It is Robert, isn't it?"

"Right. Robert Carter."

Her mother put down her teacup. "Robert came by to find out the names of a carpet cleaner and houseworker. He has to give his place a going over before he moves his furniture in."

"Shouldn't the people who own the place have—"

"Oh, yes," Libby's mother said, her lips pursed in disapproval. "They should have, but they didn't."

"My fault, probably," Robert said. "I never talked to them about the condition of the place, so I guess I have no recourse. Right now, all I want is to get the place cleaned up."

"Your landlord put her energies into gardening," Libby's mother said.

Libby glanced out the window toward the other house. Lush potato vines had been planted against trellises to separate the two units, and beyond she could see flower beds massed with color. "You'll have your hands full maintaining it," she said. She felt negative toward this man; he was interfering with her visit with her mother.

"God, I'm no gardener. When it gets too bad I'll hire somebody to come by." He grinned at her. "Your mother's full of information," he said. "She's wonderful."

Libby threw a sharp glance his way, for some reason annoyed at his praise of her mother. Good God, he wasn't going to make up to her, was he? A woman half his age?

He went on. "She's made tea for me, she's given me the name of the best carpet cleaner in town, she's even shared the name of a houseworker, which I gather is hard to come by in this community." He seemed oblivious to Libby's irritation.

Her mother returned from the kitchen with a cup for her. She poured Libby's tea.

"Your name is Libby—I don't think I know the other," Robert said.

"Altman."

"Altman! You're not Kurt's wife?"

"Yes, do you know Kurt?"

"Know him! I work for him. I've been with him for over a month now. Design. And you're his wife."

She could see him thinking: She's too young. Everyone had that initial reaction, still had it, even now that she was twenty-eight and had two children.

Her mother passed the cookies to Libby. "Did you read about that little girl?"

"The one who was killed? Yes. Terrible."

"I subbed for her English class for a whole week one time. I remember her. Bright little girl. I had them write an essay, and hers was the best in the class."

"How dreadful for you," Libby said.

"Dreadful for her?" Robert Carter sounded puzzled. "Because she subbed?"

"No, it's just that Mother is especially—sensitive to that sort of situation, especially when she knows the person. She had a close friend whose daughter was raped. The girl's never been the same."

"It ruined her life," said Libby's mother. She sighed deeply.

Libby looked at Robert Carter. His presence had suddenly become comforting. She didn't want to be alone with her mother and hear once again about her friend's daughter's rape. "How is it you're renting the place next door?" she said. "I thought owners weren't allowed to rent."

He raised a finger to his lips. "They aren't really. The cover story is that I've borrowed the place for a while. A few months ago I came back to Bay Cove from New York, where I'd been living. While I looked around for a job that would support me, I house-sat for a friend. But, alas"—he laughed—"he returned from his sabbatical leave."

"And you didn't find a job that would support you."

He grinned. "If I do some free-lance work to supplement it, *Intermission* will work out. But I was in no position to buy a house, not in this town."

"I know. Prices are insane here. You could buy an apartment on Park Avenue in New York for what you'd pay for a California bungalow."

He laughed. "Not quite, but it's bad. Do you work?" he asked.

"No, I have two small children to take care of. They're work enough. My husband"—she began and then thought, Here I go again, my secondhand identity: Kurt's work, I won't say it, and finished—"does the working."

"Gives you time to do the things you want to do. Like listen to music. Are you a music person?" Libby's mother had been forgotten. She sat sipping her tea, her eyes on nothing in particular. She's depressed, Libby thought. That little girl's started her thinking again.

"No, really more a book person," she said. "And theater and film. I like concerts, but if I had to make a choice . . ."

"I can't imagine life without music."

"Did you think of music as a career?"

"The cello, at one point. But I was a typical kid, didn't practice. Anyway, I never got good enough to do concert work. But once in a while I play with a little chamber group." He remembered his manners and turned to Libby's mother. "Mrs.—Alicia, if we bother you with our playing over there, you be sure to let me know."

Libby's mother seemed to return from a great distance. "Music doesn't bother me. It's life that bothers me." She got up heavily and walked out of the room.

Robert Carter stood up, his face anxious. "Did I—"

"No," Libby laid a hand on his sleeve. "It's that little girl. Don't mind her. She'll be all right."

"I see." She could tell that he was troubled. "Well, I'd better take my list and go. Thank your mother for me."

"Really, don't worry. In a few minutes she'll be okay. It was good talking with you. It'll be a real plus for my mother having you as a neighbor." The wistful thought went through her head that she wouldn't mind having Robert as a neighbor herself, a man her age to talk to on the evenings when Kurt worked late. Which, she commented drily to herself, seemed to be oftener and oftener.

After he had gone, she went in to her mother. Alicia lay on top of the quilt on her bed, staring at the ceiling.

Libby put a hand on hers. "Come on, Mother, don't be morbid. Come finish your tea. Do you have some brandy?"

Her mother laughed bitterly. "You think that'll make everything all right? It won't put life back in that little girl's body."

Libby sighed. "No, but let's have a shot of brandy, anyway." Clearly this was not the afternoon to discuss Kurt with her mother.

17

Meredith was too sleepy to write, but she had to write. Just a few words. She had been thinking all day about Lisa.

Wednesday, March 30

I keep wondering who could have done that thing to Lisa. All day I kept thinking about it, trying to figure it out. Jennie says she'd never have gone off with anybody she didn't know, and I think she's right. But who that she does—did, I mean—know would do such a thing? I thought of everybody we know, boys at school, even her father (that's a terrible thing to think, but I was really counting every man she knew). She didn't have any crazy uncles or cousins that I know of. It just doesn't make sense. She MUST have gone with somebody she didn't know.

Jennie says somebody told her an animal was hurt. I don't believe that. Jennie didn't know her as well as I do—I don't think she did, anyway. I think Lisa would be too smart to be taken in by that line. But then, who—and how? I hope the police find out. It would be terrible never to know.

But, it just occurred to me, it might be more terrible to know.

She was crying now. She mopped the sleeve of her nightgown across her face, hid the journal away, got into bed and turned out the light as though she were keeping someone from seeing how bad she felt.

18

The bicycle registered in Lisa Margolin's name had turned up, found by a mother who, rummaging in her garage in the process of cleaning it, had come across it: a girl's bike. She had only a son. He disclaimed all knowledge of it.

"It was tucked way back under some tarpaulins," the mother said. A fine beading of perspiration stood on her forehead. "I believe Tommy. He doesn't lie."

"Is the garage kept locked?"

"There's nothing to lock up, just junk." She twisted the fabric of her skirt. "If I'm wrong, if Tommy did have something to do with it"—she drew a ragged breath—"they wouldn't do anything to him, would they? Send him away to reform school or something?"

"No, no." Pedersen came around to her side of the desk and laid his hand on her shoulder. "He's only ten. That sort of thing sometimes happens to ten-year-old boys."

Even then, she seemed uncertain, uneasy.

Tommy was a blunt-featured towheaded youngster, dressed in rubbed jeans and a jacket unnecessarily zipped to the throat. He did not meet Pedersen's eyes. "I never saw the dumb thing before," he declared. "A *girl's* bike."

"Where'd you find it, Tommy? It's important that we know. What you might call a matter of life and death."

"A *bike*?"

"This bike."

The boy was studying his hands, tightly clasped between his knees. "What's so special about this bike?"

"It may tell us something we need to know."

He looked up. "How can a bike tell you something?"

"Did you plan to sell it? Or use parts from it?"

"I never *saw* the bike before."

Pedersen swiveled his chair around so he was facing away from the boy, looking toward the gingko tree beyond his window. He sat silent for a moment, then he swung back suddenly. "Tommy, it happens that bike was involved in a murder. Now do you see why you have to tell the truth?"

The youngster's face went white. "A *murder*?" He barely breathed the word. "I don't know anything about a *murder.*"

"Of course you don't. But you do know where that bicycle was when you picked it up. Don't you?"

The boy swallowed hard, twice. "My mother—"

"Yes, you'll have to face your parents. That'll probably be the hardest part for you. Now tell me about the bicycle."

"It was a Saturday morning. Early. It was raining out. I was supposed to meet Greg—he's my friend—in the park and I couldn't get him on the phone, so my mother said I had to put on a raincoat and go to the park and tell him I couldn't stay. Because of the rain. I was supposed to bring him home."

"The park?"

"Richards West."

"And?"

"There was nobody there. He didn't come. But I saw this bike, sort of leaning against a tree. It was all wet, as though it had been there for a while. Nobody was around, nobody. I took

it first"—he turned his face, anguished, up to Pedersen's—
"honest, I took it first because I thought I'd bring it to the police
station. I figured some girl forgot it. Then I got scared and
thought somebody'd think I stole it, so I took it home and
sneaked it into the back of the garage and covered it with some
tarps. Really, that's the truth. I wouldn't want a girl's bike. What
could I do with it?"

"Could you show me where it was if we drove you to the park?"

"In a police car? What if somebody saw me?"

"We'll take an unmarked car, a plain car like your dad's."

The boy began to cry. "They'll *kill* me."

"I don't think so. And I don't think you'll do anything like this
again—do you, Tommy?"

The boy shook his head. "What's the murder part?"

Pedersen considered. Finally he said, "I don't think we'll talk
about this, but a girl was killed. It was her bike."

"She wasn't killed because I—"

"No, no. She was dead long before you took the bike. That
had nothing to do with it." He came around and sat down next
to the boy. "Just one thing. Are you sure there was no one
around when you took the bike?"

"No, just that car. But he didn't notice me."

"What car was that?" Pedersen hoped he hadn't frightened
the boy off with the sharpness of his response.

"A car went by when I was standing there looking at the bike,
and then it came by again when I was walking the bike away.
It sort of scared me, but I could see the guy wasn't paying any
attention to me."

"Did you get a look at the man?"

"No, I just looked up and he was gone."

"Did he seem to be looking for something or someone?"

"No. I think maybe he turned wrong, and he was going back
where he came from. He was looking straight ahead."

"You saw him enough to see that?"

"I didn't really. I just looked up and he was gone. I mean, I'd
have noticed if he was looking at me. I was feeling sort of—"

"Guilty? What kind of car was it?"

But it was no use. He couldn't remember.

Pedersen stood up. "Come on now. Here's a tissue. Blow your nose and go tell your mother she can go home."

L ater, he said to Tate, "It was pretty much what we thought. She parked the bike against the tree near the path where she was seen. Didn't even chain it. Just went off down the path with her murderer."

"If the kid hadn't taken it—"

"She'd have been found earlier. But anyway, now we don't have to go on assuming the murderer has it stashed away somewhere. I don't like that business of the car. On the way to the park, I questioned the boy some more. He couldn't even remember what color it was."

"Too preoccupied with his own guilt."

"I think so. And it may very well have been someone who just turned off by mistake and was going back." Pedersen paused. "Sean drives a car."

"He's licensed. They were out of town that Saturday."

"I know. I talked to him yesterday. He professes complete ignorance. Lisa is just some kid his sister knew."

"If it was the murderer returning, that means the murderer is clearly not Sean."

"We don't know it was the murderer. It's just one more bit of confusion to add to the rest. You know, Ron, maybe we'd better see what we can scout out about pedophilia. If we could do a profile on this guy, it might help."

"Right up my alley. I'll see what I can find."

"One thing that keeps bothering me."

"The pulled-up jeans."

"Yes. Bothers you, too?"

"It's odd. The guy must have been in a panic because she fought him or because he killed her. You'd think he'd be desperate to get away from that park."

"Yes. So what does that tell us about him?"

"He regretted it? Either the attempted rape or the murder."

"Or he knew her and couldn't bear to leave her that way, exposed."

"A sensitive killer? Maybe he just wanted to call less attention to her. The dark jeans, the green jacket—"

"Yes." Pedersen leaned back in his chair. "Maybe all of those."

"If it was her friend's brother—"

"You think he'd be concerned about how she looked to other people? Maybe. But the brother was on his way to Sonoma. Unless, of course, he killed her before he left. I keep thinking—"

"According to the time given us by those two women at the pool, the swim class was over around a quarter of four. The Cranes left around four-thirty. Tight, but possible."

"What about the men at *Intermission*? Did you double-check on their whereabouts that afternoon?"

"Yes, right after you told me. Syd Pagano was in the field, he thought he was talking with Redwood Realty about then; they said he came in sometime in the late afternoon. Kurt Altman thought he was in his office, wasn't sure. Robert Carter had been talking with the photographer that's doing the magazine covers; he was out of the office. The photographer confirmed that he came in that afternoon, couldn't say exactly when."

"And Joel Sterne?"

"He was working at home, alone. None of those guys very much appreciated our interest in them. Carter and Altman were really put out."

"And what did we learn? Any of them could have done it. Well, get what you can on pedophilia. We'll go from there." Pedersen rose and went to stand by the window. "I just can't get my teeth into this case, Ron. It sickens me. The idea of that being done to a kid—and that bright little girl, with her poems and her neat room and her dog Taffy. I don't know. I guess I have what the psychoanalysts call a block."

Ronald Tate stood up to go. "I know. I'll see what I can find. I'll get back to you." He stopped at the door. "We'll work it out. We just need time. And some information."

After he left, Carl Pedersen said to the empty room, "Damn it to hell, I hope so." He felt tired.

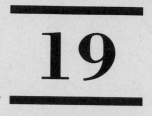

19

It amused Libby. She worried about Ruth's happiness, and Ruth fussed over her. Currently, Ruth was convinced Libby wasn't getting enough from Kurt. She questioned Libby about what had attracted her to him, a man so many years older—questioned her cautiously, Libby noted, so her friend wouldn't take offense. And it was true: she *had* been young, a gangly, childlike girl, to have been drawn to a man eighteen years her senior, old enough to be her father. She knew that even now she had the lean, leggy look of a girl, and she moved in an energetic rush, like someone years younger. But she had been perfectly contented—oh, a little impatient for the children to be more grown so she could return to school or work—but happy. That was, until lately. Now there was the sex, the absence of it. There was a sort of tedium that was creeping in; Kurt seemed forever to be watching TV or busy in his study, unavailable to her. And there was the business of that woman she had seen with him.

Divorce had even crossed her mind once or twice. That was

crazy. Even in a worst-case scenario, if things had been much grimmer than they were, divorce would solve nothing. She'd just be left with full care of the kids, Kurt unable to give her enough support money, bringing up two daughters yearning for a daddy as she had yearned. Just any job to supplement income, indifferent day care—all the problems that went with single motherhood. Sometimes Libby wondered why people had children at all, they complicated life so.

And things weren't that bad. She'd just sit tight and ride it out. But it did seem unfair. She was still in her twenties, and although maybe she had been looking for her lost father when she married Kurt, she had been looking for a husband, too. Ruth was right: he didn't give her enough.

But of course Ruth's concern over her was influenced by her own life. Since Joel she had been different, happier. Happy. Ruth's interest in her marriage had to do with thoughts about marriage for herself. Ruth was beginning to think it wouldn't be so bad being with Joel full time. Libby sighed. At least they were the right ages for each other. And had a good sex life. And were interested only in each other.

B ut by the weekend Libby had once again convinced herself she was mistaken: it was merely a man that looked like Kurt whom she had seen enter the apartment house on Ash Street. She spent Friday more happily domestic than she had been in a long time, making beds, vacuuming, marketing for seafood for chowder, buying cut flowers, picking up the children. She found herself cheered, though she wasn't sure whether by her change of mind regarding Kurt or because of the appreciative glint she had caught in Robert Carter's eye when she talked with him at her mother's. He had crossed her mind more than once since Wednesday. There was nothing, she decided, like being admired by an attractive man to lift a woman's spirits. So when Kurt came home with his news, her reaction was mixed.

Kurt had been looking well lately, a little tired, but well. At forty-six, despite his air of boyishness, he had a solidity that added stature and authority to his appearance. His hair was still dark and he had the tanned, healthy look of a man who spends time out-of-doors; in fact, the tan had been acquired under a sunlamp. After seven years of marriage, there was no diminution of his physical appeal for her.

"Well," he said, tossing his jacket over a chair and settling on a kitchen stool next to the sink where she was washing lettuce for salad. "My new graphics man and I are going after the magazine: new format, better paper, clever illustrations, more photographs."

She was surprised. "The man you hired a month ago?"

"Yes. From New York—at least he's been working there for a couple of years. But originally he was local, so he has a feel for the community. Of course the place has changed while he's been away, the same as it changed while we lived in San Francisco, but having someone local with New York experience—"

"That's what the publisher said about you. Someone local with San Francisco experience. Your graphic man's name is Robert Carter?"

"He'll take over the—" Kurt stopped in midsentence. "Yes. Why? Do you know him?"

"If it's Robert Carter, I do. He took the mobile home next to Mother's."

Kurt frowned. "Funny place for him to be living. When did you meet him?"

"Oh, a week or so ago. Then when I dropped by there the other day he was at Mother's getting the name of carpet cleaners. She'd taken him under her wing, like one of her students."

"Did he say anything about the job?"

"No, he did say he'd been looking for the right one. I guess he found it." Something oddly proprietary in her was disturbed that Robert should be one of Kurt's staff.

"Hmm. Well, anyway, we spent most of today mapping strategy for the first new issue."

86

"He seems like a nice guy."

"Yes. He's twenty-seven, a year younger than you, but he's one of those bright young men I keep bumping into that run the world these days. Makes me feel a million years old." He grinned. "Why aren't you out there, heading up a law firm or running a brokerage house? You're not living up to your generation."

"Give me a couple of years. As soon as Cory's in school—"

"Hey," he said, "I'm kidding. You don't have to prove yourself to me."

"Maybe not to you, but to me. I have a plan, too, just as you have one for the magazine. I'm not wild about full-time housekeeping, you know. So, what are you going to change?"

He leaned back against the counter, crunching a piece of endive he had removed from the salad bowl. "We're going to use discrete sections, have clear-cut music, art, theater, film sections, with glossy dividers. We're going to add a section on restaurants, not just local, county, but with emphasis on Bay Cove. Interviews with owners, comments by diners, that sort of thing. We're going to draw on local paintings for our covers, maybe even for our dividers. And we're going to add an opinion section: pertinent letters from our readers and editorial comment." She could see he was high on his plan.

"You're doing a lot, you're turning it into a full-blown magazine."

"It's a full-blown magazine now; it just doesn't have that sort of delineation. And we'll expand it slightly, of course. Slightly for now, at least. Maybe more extensively once we see how the advertisers cotton to our new format. And"—he paused—"we'll charge for it. Take subscriptions."

"And all this is Robert's idea?"

He looked at her sharply. "No, it's not all Carter's idea; it's something we've worked out together." After a pause he added, "Maybe you'd better not be so friendly with him till we get established together."

"Oh, come off it." She plunked the salad bowl on the table. "I don't have any publishing secrets to protect. Besides, I met him on my own; it has nothing to do with you. Get the girls, will you?"

He rose. "Well, just don't go carrying things from me to him. Things I say at home about the magazine are between us. Probably you won't see anything of him, anyway."

She found she was annoyed. "Oh, I might. He and Mother have become good friends." Kurt seemed unthreatened by the idea that this younger, attractive male was among her acquaintances. Did he think no one other than he ever looked at her?

As though Kurt sensed her irritation and its source, he said, "Well, don't go getting too friendly with him." He paused beside her. "Keep your mind on the children."

Mollified, she squeezed him. "I will. I do." She sighed. "To the exclusion of all else. Where the hell are they? Get them, Kurt, will you, before everything's ice cold?"

As she settled the girls in their chairs, she said, "Does this new format mean a lot of extra hours? Night work?"

"It may. For just a little while. I have to go back tonight."

"Tonight! The Bruces are coming by, did you forget? And that man from work. Syd Pagano."

"Shit, I did." He raised one hand. That's all right, I'll make a couple of phone calls, its nothing urgent. We can work on it tomorrow."

"If that's so, why did you plan to work tonight? Damn it, I don't understand you, Kurt. Do you think I *like* spending my evenings by myself? It's bad enough being here all day—with all the stimulation a five-year-old has to offer."

"Now don't get exercised about it. I'll try to keep the extra hours at a minimum, and I said I'd do something about tonight. Don't let's start the evening with a fight."

"It's not my doing. If you remembered your social obligations—"

He groaned. "Shit. We're going to have it, aren't we?"

With an effort she made her voice pleasant. "No. We're not. Let's let it go. It's your night to bathe the kids. While you're getting them to bed, I'll throw something together for tonight. Brownies, I guess." She smiled at the children. "You get your old man tonight."

"Old man," said Cory cheerfully, beaming at her father.

"Good!" said Kate.

"I'll remember that, Kate," Libby said. "I'll remember your faithlessness." Kate, who knew she was being teased but was not sure about what, looked at her mother uncertainly.

"It's all right, Katy." Libby laughed and rumpled her daughter's hair. "I know you like Daddy to bathe you."

"Sure you do, muffin, don't you?" Kurt said.

Libby glanced over at him, wondering how he could be so appealing and so irritating at one and the same time.

Libby was rinsing the dishes when Kurt made his phone calls. Or call. It sounded like just one. She turned off the water and listened.

"—can't make it tonight. I forgot we have friends coming by."

There was a long silence during which apparently he just listened. "Look," he said, "we'll talk about it when I see you. I can't discuss it now. Sorry about tonight." He sounded angry. "Well, I can't help it. I'm sorry, I said."

It struck her, as she turned on the water again, that it was an odd way for Kurt to have spoken to Robert. Maybe she'd ask Robert what it was all about when, and if, she saw him. She smiled to herself. Kurt didn't own him, after all.

20

Meredith entered her room quietly since her mother was still asleep. And Sean, probably. On Saturdays he slept half the day. She balanced the bowl of Grapenut Flakes on the pile of books that stood on her desk and opened the half-gallon container of milk. After she had poured milk on her cereal, she parked the milk container on the floor to one side of the desk and returned to her unmade bed to fish the journal from beneath the mattress. Smiling slightly, she established herself at the desk, where she could alternately eat and write.

Saturday, April 2

It's Saturday morning and I don't have any place I have to be and my homework is finished. *I can't believe I did it all last night, but Mother was listening to some dumb radio program on AIDS and she was in a terrible mood. I thought it was best that I stay in my room, and I'd just finished that new Judy Blume so I figured I might as well get my homework out of the way. Maybe I'll do that every week. It feels so good not to have it hanging over my head. (But I know I won't. I have these times when I'm full of good resolutions and I keep my room clean and my homework caught up and then, suddenly, for no reason, everything's in a mess again. I don't understand it.)*

After I finished the homework, I read—reread, really—a little of Anne's diary. If I could go anywhere in the world, I'd want to go to Amsterdam. You can go right into the house she lived in and climb up into the attic and go in her room. A friend of mine went with her family. She said there were pictures of movie stars on the walls that Anne and her sister had cut out of magazines. And a map her father had marked with what was happening in the war. And she said when the wall was shut up, you couldn't tell there was a door there at all. She could feel Anne there in the room and she cried. One thing, she said they must have had to keep very quiet. That must have been horrible. Imagine Mother and Sean and me keeping quiet for the whole day. Especially Sean.

Though Sean doesn't say so much. Actually he acts kind of weird. Sometimes I think he's a little crazy from all the dope he does. He came in my room the other night and lay down on my bed and just lay there for the longest time, not saying a word. Then all of a sudden he asked me the craziest question. He said, "Do you and your friends ever put out for anyone?" I couldn't think what he meant, and then he laughed and said, "Go the whole way, dummy?" He was looking at me in the strangest way, as though—I don't know what. I got up and yelled, really yelled, out loud so my mother could hear it, "You just get out of here with your dirty mind!" He kind of sneered but he got up and went out of my room. Yikes! I don't understand him anymore. It doesn't seem like he was ever my big brother that used to take care of me and was so sweet. He certainly isn't sweet anymore. What a weirdo!

She reread the passages for spelling and closed the book. Once again she experienced the sick feeling she had had when Sean had asked her the question, when he got that strange look on his face. Sean did need a father, just as her mother said. She needed one, too, although her mother never talked about *that*. A queer sense of longing came over her when she thought of her father; she could never understand how he could divorce even his children, but it seemed he had. She wouldn't be able to do that if she ever had children, just forget about them because he had a new wife. She hadn't forgotten *him* just because he didn't live with them anymore; she could picture his face, his funny, cozy smile when they had a secret, even his expression when he was mad, the cold mask that dropped over his face that was usually so friendly.

She sighed. Sean needed him more than she did, she supposed, being a boy and all. Sometimes she wondered if she should even be alone in the house with her brother.

21

Saturday morning over a leisurely second cup of coffee—
Kurt had taken the children with him on an errand—Libby
reviewed the evening before. It had been strange, mostly
because of Syd. Syd, as a matter of fact, was a strange man.
Good-looking—God, he was good-looking—and sexy, but
strange. Libby couldn't put her finger on the source of his
oddness—maybe his rather dour demeanor, as though he didn't
find much pleasure in life.

The Bruces, who had never before met him, tried to involve
him in conversation and finally gave up and chattered on about
things concerning their own lives. They had a new baby—Patty
Bruce was rather old to have just started a family—and they
thought him the most remarkable creature on the face of the
earth; therefore, they had dozens of completely predictable
stories about the child. Libby found her attention wandering
back to Syd, who sat with a polite, rather stiff smile, as though
he were enduring their ecstacies. Eventually, the Bruces ran

down and Libby turned to Syd. "You aren't married, I gather, Syd."

He shook his head. "Not at the moment. I was."

"Any kids?"

"No, no kids."

"Then," she said, "all these stories about our children must be pretty dull for you."

"Not dull. I just don't connect very well with them. I like kids well enough, but I like them better when they reach the age of reason."

Everyone but Syd laughed.

"Syd," Kurt said, "that laughter comes from our conviction that children never reach the age of reason."

"That may be," said Syd. "Anyway, when they get to an age where they have some intellectual curiosity, they interest me more. You know"—he looked at his watch—"I hate like hell to do this, but I have to be on my way. I'm expecting a long-distance call around ten-thirty. Don't let me break things up, though, I'll just sort of sidle out." For the first time he smiled. He had a wonderful smile.

Libby rose. "You needn't sidle out, Syd. I'll even walk you to the door. It won't break things up." She almost wished it would. It was becoming clearer with every visit that the Bruces should be put on hold socially until they had gotten past this period of adulation of their child. She wasn't sure she herself could endure too many more sessions like this evening. Certainly she sympathized with Syd's need to escape.

Kurt too accompanied Syd to the door, waving the Bruces, who had risen, back to their seats. When he and Libby returned, he said, "I asked him because he seems sort of lonely—a loner, at any rate. Funny guy, though."

"He seems depressed," Patty Bruce said.

"Yes. Or preoccupied. Maybe he's in the throes of some big affair we don't know about."

"Long distance," said Libby.

"He's wonderful looking," Patty said. "So sexy."

"He is," Libby agreed, "but it's as though something's missing. Except when he smiles. He sort of comes to life when he smiles. Funny, though, I can't imagine being attracted to him."

"You'd better not be," Kurt said, and laughed. "What about something to eat? Shall I send out for pizza?" The discussion of Syd was at an end.

The night work set in almost at once. Libby, trying to be reasonable, said nothing at first, but after the third evening of sitting alone before the television set, she protested.

Kurt was not responsive to her complaints. "Listen, Lib," he said, "we're overhauling the whole fucking magazine—you can't think that doesn't take work. Carter and I have only evenings—all day long, it's one interruption after another. Bear with me, kid, it won't be forever."

She hadn't thought it would be forever. "What is it you're doing, exactly? You had the thing all mapped out from day one. What more is there to do?"

He sighed deeply, as though she were a burden he found heavy. "In a general way, we had it mapped out. In fact, it takes a lot of very careful selection before we hit on just what we want."

"Selection of what?" She stood up, seeing her angry face reflected in the oval Danish mirror they had bought together the first year they were married. She looked pretty with her hair tousled where she had run her hands through it; she wore no makeup, only the pink cheeks of her anger. Her appearance didn't comfort her. Once more, the tucked-away suspicion of him surfaced. "You're sure you *are* at work?"

"Where else would I be? Sit down, will you? Don't *pace*. Do you think I like to put in hours like these?"

"Selection of what?"

"What? Oh, typefaces, papers, prints for our dividers, that sort of thing. The magazine doesn't just put itself together, you know. It takes time. We'd like to make the changes for the next issue, if we can." He sat down and for the first time she noticed that his face was drawn. He did look tired.

95

Pulling a hassock over to his chair, she sat down before him, her face turned toward his. "I'm sorry. I'll try to stop griping. I'm sure once it's done, it'll be done and you won't work evenings. But, Kurt, you have no idea how . . . boring it can be around kids all day when you have nothing to look forward to in the evening. If I worked or went to school or something . . . I adore the kids but, really, they aren't exactly intellectual companions."

"I wish *I* could stay home and take care of them. I wouldn't find it boring."

"Oh, yes, you would, if you were honest about it. If I have to read *The Elephant's Child* one more time—for that matter, if I have to explain to Kate and Cory where you are one more time . . . I'm sorry, I'm doing it again."

He stayed home the next night, and they made love. But the following evening he phoned again, apologetic. He would have to be late.

L ibby lifted the receiver. The children were bedded down and the sitter was coming by, bringing her homework. She was damned if she'd sit around stewing for another evening. She'd call her mother and see if she'd like to take in a movie.

There was no answer at her mother's house.

Pulling the car out of the driveway, she turned it toward downtown; there was a new French film at the Barnhouse. Then she hesitated. It was odd that her mother shouldn't be in. She was mildly alarmed; her mother seldom went out in the evening. Perhaps she should just detour past. No harm in that.

The house was dark. Libby slowed. Could she have gone to a movie? She couldn't remember her mother having gone to a movie except with her in years. She pulled the car up and went to the door. Really, she should have a key—this was crazy, worrying that something might have happened to her mother and having no way to get in and check. No one answered her knock or the ringing of the bell.

Next door, Robert Carter's house glowed with light. Funny, Kurt had said they'd be working late. She circled around and walked up the path between the primroses the owner had planted, their vivid colors lighted by the porch lamp. Robert came to the door. He wore a sweatshirt and jeans and moccasins. From behind him poured recorded sounds of a chamber group.

He looked pleased. "Hi, Libby. Come to see whether I'm settled in?"

"No." She found she was suddenly self-conscious. "I'm sure you are, but I came to see if you have any idea where my mother is. I suppose you don't."

"As a matter of fact, you're right, I don't. I'm sure she's fine. Probably gone to a movie. I saw her around dinner time. She was out in the yard."

Her mother forgotten, Libby said, "Dinner time? I thought you and Kurt were working tonight."

He stood back from the door. "Come on in. I really am settled and presentable."

She followed him in. He was settled. The room had been painted white. In lieu of a sofa, he had placed several black canvas director's chairs in a ring around a low round coffee table. Beneath it lay a colorful Indian Numdah rug. In one corner fat cushions covered in navy and white Indonesian fabric were stacked. Rice paper shades covered the windows; several handsome line drawings had been framed and hung on the walls. "You've made the place look marvelous," she said. "You have a real flair." She walked over to one of the drawings. "Your own?" she asked.

He nodded. "You like them?" He turned down the stereo.

"I do. I see why Kurt was so glad to get you." She continued to stand with her back to him. "You're lucky to get away tonight, Kurt's still there. But I guess you've worked almost every evening this week. That's no way to treat a new employee. Such a talented employee." She wondered if she sounded patronizing, the boss's wife speaking. She faced him. "I mean—"

"I'm glad you think I'm talented, but Kurt hasn't been

overworking me. I've stayed an extra hour or two a couple of times, that's all. Some things to tie up. It's hard during the day."

"Yes. Still, an extra hour or two—that breaks in on dinner time. You must be famished when you get out. Or do you and Kurt have something sent in?"

"No, no, nothing like that. I've been home by seven every night. I can wait for my dinner till seven, I'm a big boy." He looked amused.

She felt her face grow warm. Sitting down, barely knowing what she said, she asked, "What sorts of things do you do? Choose typefaces, things like that?"

He looked at her thoughtfully, as though it were beginning to dawn on him why she was asking. "Well," he said carefully, "yes. Actually we selected the typefaces earlier, but there are other things." He rose. "How about a drink? I have a bottle of white wine just opened."

"Lovely." She leaned back in the canvas chair and closed her eyes for a moment. When he returned with the glasses, she said, "When I came, you must have been doing something. I interrupted you."

"It's an interruption I appreciate." He touched her glass with his. "To—what shall I say? The beginning of a beautiful friendship?" He grinned. "I'd like that."

She couldn't take her eyes off his. "Yes. To . . . friendship."

He laughed. "Not quite what I said, but it'll do. You're worried about Kurt, is that it? He's working too hard?"

She was unable to lie. "I don't know. I don't even know if he's working at all. Evenings, I mean."

"He's always hard at it when I leave," said Robert loyally.

She leaned toward him. "Sometimes, Robert—is that what I call you? Or Bob?"

"Robert."

"Sometimes, Robert, I think he's having some sort of fling, an affair." She heard herself. She was telling a virtual stranger, and an employee of Kurt's, something she had barely mentioned to her best friend. She let her voice become light, amused. "Shows how too steady a dose of kids can make you crazy. A couple weeks ago I was sure I saw him over on Ash Street one afternoon, when actually he hadn't stepped away from the magazine all day. Hallucinating. Crazy."

He smiled. "I'm sure you're not crazy. I wouldn't know, not having been married, but I imagine wives, and husbands, too, go through these times when they . . . doubt each other."

"Kurt never acts as though he doubts me." She said it with resentment.

"That's a compliment, isn't it?"

She felt the wine relaxing her. "Maybe that's the answer. Maybe I should give him reason to." She heard herself with dismay. What was she trying to do, seduce this nice man who was trying so hard to reassure her? "I didn't mean that the way it sounded."

He waved a hand dismissively. "I'm sure that's *not* the solution. Have you told Kurt how worried you are?"

She laughed. "I can see you haven't been married."

He looked confused. "If a marriage is good—"

"If it's good, you don't make it better by behaving like the jealous little woman." She realized she was picking up even Kurt's way of expressing things. "Jealous wife. No, either I have to trust Kurt or not trust him." It sounded so easy.

Suddenly he stood up and went to the window, drawing back a corner of the shade. "There. I thought I heard her. Your mother's home." He turned back to her. "I didn't mean that the way it sounded, either." He smiled. "I'd love you to stay all evening, but now at least you can relax about her."

"Shows how little I know about people. Even my own mother. I thought she never went to the movies at night without me."

He laughed, a little sadly. "I guess we don't know much about anyone. Perhaps that's the reason you're unsure of Kurt."

"You're saying we need to get acquainted—after seven years of marriage?"

"Maybe."

"He has a whole hidden self I don't know?" She laughed wryly.

"Don't be angry. He may have. You may have. I may have. It's hard to know anyone, really."

"Is that why you're not married?"

He laughed, relieving the tension she felt. "No. I guess you might say I'm waiting for the right woman to appear." His brow wrinkled. "I'm young, you know."

She had a sudden impulse to go over and hug him. She stood up abruptly. "Really, I must go. I should be sure everything's okay with Mother and then get on home. Kurt must be there by now." She put out her hand. "Thanks for the wine and the shoulder. I didn't mean to take advantage of you."

He continued to hold her hand. His own was smooth, silky, the hand of a man who does not do hard work. She looked down at it. For a moment she could imagine the blunt, spatulate artist's hand cupping her chin, caressing her face. She jerked her hand free. This man disturbed her. She wanted to get out of his house.

22

"How's it going?" Freda asked. She was removing a casserole from the oven. "Everything's ready. You can sit down."

"How's what going? You mean the Lisa Margolin case?"

"Mmm. Be careful of this casserole now; it's hot. Yes, the Lisa Margolin killing."

"It's not going anywhere. We've reached a dead end."

She sat down. "Give me your plate. Funny how something like that can happen and no one sees or hears anything. People are so inquisitive, usually."

"When they see something that isn't as it should be. The thing about this is that it must have appeared perfectly normal. They—Lisa and her attacker—must have seemed completely ordinary. Not worth noticing."

"Doesn't that lead to some conclusions?"

"You mean the guy looked old enough to be her father—they looked like father and daughter?"

"Yes. Or brother and sister, if he was younger."

"Her friend has a brother, you know. A very peculiar character. He may just be going through a rather—thorny adolescence. Or he may be on dope. Or he may just be strange."

"You told me about him. Is he a suspect, a real one?"

"We have no reason to think that. He just came to mind when you mentioned brother and sister."

"What about those men you told me you saw at the magazine?"

"Nobody seems to know anything. None of them seemed in the least uneasy—moved, of course, but anybody would be over the death of a child, a bright little girl like that. But not uneasy. No, we're no place." He sighed. "This is good. What's this in with the chicken, artichoke hearts?"

"Yes, it's a new recipe. I get so sick of chicken. So what are you going to do? Not just wait, are you, Carl?"

"We've followed up everything we could. We're keeping an eye out, don't worry, and the park and shore drive are both being patrolled regularly. It's just that we haven't a damned thing that's solid. If the man had raped her—I told you he didn't?"

She nodded.

"We'd have had something. All we have is a question—why didn't he rape her? Obviously that's what he took her into the bushes for?"

"Maybe he couldn't."

"That's not usual with rapists. Unfortunately, they can."

"She fought so hard he thought someone would hear?"

"That's possible. So hard he panicked and just wanted to hush her up. That's what we're assuming."

"But you said he had—covered her up again."

He grinned at her. "You're becoming quite a detective yourself. Yes, that's at odds with the panic idea. If he was hysterical with fear, he'd have got out of there fast. It's a case with a lot of contradictions."

"And you didn't find anything?"

"A crumpled elementary school arithmetic paper. A crushed Coke can. And a thin piece of bamboo, hollow."

"Could it have been used for cocaine?"

"It could have, but it didn't show any evidence of coke. What can you think of that's made of bamboo?"

Freda looked at him thoughtfully. "Just a minute."

She returned a minute later, carrying a bright furled parasol. "Look at this." The parasol had tiny hollow spokes of bamboo. "Was it like this?"

Pedersen took the parasol from her hands. "This is the closest we've come. But why would the guy be carrying a parasol?"

"Maybe she was."

"A *paper* parasol in the rain?"

"I see what you mean. You said they looked ordinary."

He laughed. "That's right." He returned to his dinner. A moment passed and he said again, "Why would she have been carrying a paper parasol? No, that can't be it."

After a while he murmured, "You know, Freda, don't ask me about this case anymore."

23

Meredith listened to be sure her mother wasn't calling her—she wasn't; she was talking to Sean—and walked over to her bed. Sliding her hand between box springs and mattress, she reached for her journal. Nothing met her touch. Startled, she slid her hand further in. Nothing. Panic welled in her, then her fingers brushed something. Poked way back almost out of her reach was the diary, its pages crumpled. She smoothed them, controlling an impulse to race through the house shouting accusations. Her mother? Sean? It must be Sean. Her mother would have been careful to put it back just so; she'd never have known it had been touched if it had been her mother who read it. It was Sean. That fink! That *weirdo*! After what had happened the other evening, she'd think he'd stay clear of her.

She leafed through the journal, reading it as though she were her brother. Except for the references to him and to her menstruation, there was nothing terribly private, but still she didn't like the idea that he'd read it. She checked the door and sat down to write.

Thursday, April 7

That weirdo brother of mine has read my journal.

She thought, I just might as well give him something to read, in case he finds it again. This time, though, she'd hide it so he wouldn't find it. She went on.

He put it back all wrong and I could tell right away. You'd think he'd have something more important to do than to snoop in what isn't his business! From now on I'll be careful what I put in this journal.

It started out being a terrible day. It was as though all of a sudden I realized—really realized—that Lisa was gone, and every time I turned a corner at school, I remembered something about her, something we'd done together or some poem she'd written or something funny she'd said. Finally I went into the john and closed myself in one of the booths and just bawled. Why did somebody have to kill Lisa?

But it seems as though every time I have something awful to write, I have something good, too. After school I was feeling too bad to come home and face Sean, so I went down to the mall. I was just walking along, looking at windows, when I ran into (I'm not going to use names from now on, in case Sean gets at this again) one of my new friends. I was standing in front of Things and All, looking at a window full of plastic objects to show what can be made from plastic, and HE came up beside me. Then he looked my way and said, "Well, what a nice surprise!" I think I blushed a little. I'm not used to grown-ups acting as though I'm a nice surprise, but he asked me what I thought of the window, just as though I were another adult, and he listened to my answer. (I notice a lot of adults ask you questions and then don't pay attention to what you answer.) After we talked about the

105

window, I turned to go and he said, "Do you have some free time?" I didn't have to be anyplace, so I said, "Sure, why?" and he said, "I thought maybe you'd like to go across the street to Kettle House and have a drink of some sort. Tea? Lemonade?"

Anyway, that's what we did. We sat outside on the patio and he ordered us both iced tea and some little cakes and we sat and talked, just like two adults. (I'm trying not to say grown-ups all the time.) He told me some things about himself, which I won't put in here because of Sean, including that he is shy like I am. I never thought men were shy.

While we had tea, I asked him about Lisa, if he knew her. He looked at me oddly. I think he didn't know what I was talking about, and said, "Lisa?" I said, "The girl I came to the magazine with." "Oh," he said, "the girl who was killed. That was terrible. No I didn't know her. Should I have?" I had to smile, he looked so bewildered. I said, "No, I just thought you might have seen her again somewhere." "No," he said. "Just the once." And he sighed, and then we talked about something else. So there, Mr. Detective, I told you he was innocent!

When we got up to go, he shook hands with me and said he'd had a lovely time. I practically floated home, I was so excited. But when I got there, there was no one to tell. I couldn't very well tell my mother, for obvious reasons, and I certainly wouldn't tell Sean, and Jennie wasn't home. (Afterwards I was glad. I think I won't tell Jennie about this.) I'll probably never see him again like that, but it was fun. It felt like a date with Daddy. I haven't had a real date yet, just gone places with a bunch of kids, but this was different.

Now I'm going to find a hiding place for this book that Sean can't possibly find.

She stood in the middle of the room, the journal clasped between her palms, and thought. Where? Where could she put it that Sean wouldn't look? The closet was too obvious; the bookcase wouldn't do because the red of the cover would be noticeable. She slid her eyes over the dresser, the desk, the bed, the hamper. The hamper! That was it; Sean would never rummage around among her dirty clothes to find it; he'd never even think of it. She didn't much like putting the precious volume in among grubby jeans and night dresses she had worn, but she took a clean pair of panties from her dresser drawer, wrapped the diary in it, and buried it at the very bottom of the hamper. She wondered if she'd be able to tell if Sean found it again. Could she keep a thread or something at the top of the stack of soiled clothes? No, that was silly, the thread would be disturbed every time she forgot and tossed something in or took things out to wash them. She'd just have to take her chances.

Once more she checked to see just how she had folded the panties around the diary, then she returned it to the hamper and piled the clothes over it. Closing the hamper, it occurred to her that it was pretty crazy that she had to sneak around like this in her own house. In her own *room*.

24

"The profile," said Ronald Tate. He opened his notebook. "First of all," he said, "pedophilia frequently begins in middle age. But"—he added quickly as Pedersen opened his mouth to speak—"it can begin anytime in adulthood, including late adolescence."

Pedersen said, "Well, that covers the entire population. Great."

Tate ignored him. "Usually it's a chronic problem, but often the severity fluctuates"—he looked at his notes—"with psychosocial stress. Isolated sexual acts may be"—he read— "'precipitated by marital discord, recent loss or intense loneliness.'" He looked up. "As a substitute for a preferred but unavailable adult, for example."

"What about the age of the child?"

"If the individual is an adult, the kids are usually at least ten years younger. If the individual is a late adolescent, there's no particular age difference." He glanced again at his notes.

"Recidivism is high, not so high as with homosexually oriented pedophiles." He dropped the notebook on Pedersen's desk.

"You did your homework. But what did it get us?"

"I forgot. The pedophile finds adult women threatening."

"Some overwhelming woman in his past? A mother or sister or aunt?"

"Probably. Or grandmother. Someone who brought him up. At any rate he seeks out little girls who seem to pose no threat. He doesn't feel overwhelmed by them. In fact, he may feel quite tender toward them, only want to touch or look. Usually older adults look for eight- or ten-year-olds."

Pedersen gave a grunt of disgust. "Except this kid—Lisa—looked like a ten-year-old. She may have been mature beyond her years, but to look at, she was a skinny, breastless little girl."

"So if we published a profile, we'd be all over the scene?"

"It looks that way. Any age from sixteen to—whatever. Sixty, I guess. Married or—are they married?"

"The older ones often are. Or were."

"It's no use," said Pedersen. "We'd do better to publish another warning, an urgent one—beware of all friendly men of all ages, don't go for walks or rides anywhere, even if you know the man—"

"Yes. I forgot to mention that most incidents are initiated by adults who are a part of—how did they put it? A part of the 'intimate interpersonal environment of the child,' I think it was."

Let's do that, then. Let's have the newspapers carry another strong warning and maybe post some fliers around town. State that it may be someone they know—a young person or a much older one—that he may be very friendly and gentle. Scare the kids a little. We've got to frighten them into a little caution." He rubbed his hand across his eyes. "What are we doing to our kids these days? Having to teach them to anticipate—"

"Evil?"

"Yes, evil! At every turn."

"It isn't like when you brought up kids, Carl. Times have changed."

"Damned straight, they have." He struck the desk with his palm.

The younger man leaned toward him. "Calm down, Carl. We're doing all we can."

Pedersen glared. "I don't feel calm." After a moment he said thoughtfully, "Do you think that factor of psychosocial stress applies here? We have the kid, the brother of the friend, who's just lost a father. There's the possibility of marital discord with Altman; we can't know. The other two guys—Sterne and Carter—may be feeling pretty lost and lonely; they haven't been back in Bay Cove for long, and probably old friends have moved on. And Pagano struck me as the smooth, glib sort of man who makes superficial relationships; underneath, he may be lonely as hell."

Tate laughed. "That certainly covers it."

Pedersen looked amused. "It does, doesn't it? But what I mean is that any of them could be suffering psychosocial stress and we wouldn't know it."

"Most of us are. Most of the time."

Pedersen looked at his partner with irritation and changed the subject. "I've been thinking about that crumpled arithmetic paper. We treated it pretty lightly, but it could have been dropped by a school teacher."

"Maybe, but remember there was no name, teacher or child. Nothing. No way to identify who it belonged to."

"And the problem with that is that it's an *elementary* school paper. Lisa would have had contact with junior high school teachers. Besides, the Margolins made no mention of a teacher who was a friend, except for the university people. I guess it's a crazy idea. The bamboo's a better likelihood."

"If we knew what it was."

"Freda thought it looked as though it came from a Japanese umbrella she had. I don't think so. It just doesn't fit. It looked to me more like part of a chopstick. I checked out bamboo blinds; they're made of flat pieces, this was hollow."

"Maybe none of those things we found have any connection."

"Maybe not."

"Don't get discouraged. Something'll pop up when we least expect it."

"Aren't you discouraged, Ron? We don't come up with anything solid. And there's that damned business—I just can't remember what someone said at that magazine when we went there. It was pertinent, I know, but it keeps eluding me."

"It'll come back. Those things always do. You looked over those notes I took?"

"I did. It couldn't have seemed important or you'd have jotted something down."

"I didn't take down every word, but I think I got the major information."

"No. I think whatever it was was said in passing, the sort of thing no one notes down."

"Relax. Forget it. That works best for me."

Pedersen looked at his partner and grinned. "You must think what I need is not another detective but a therapist. You've done a lot of reassuring this morning."

"You do the same for me." Ronald Tate stood up to go. "You're the last man I'd recommend to a therapist. You just don't like crimes against children."

"No. You can say that again. Several times."

25

The journal had remained undisturbed. Meredith, unsure as to whether Sean's interest had waned or whether he'd been unable to find her hiding place, was satisfied that it was being read by no one. Nevertheless, she continued to be careful.

Friday, April 8

Today HE called.
I'd better begin at the beginning. It was a school day and I was feeling sort of sad. I'd had lunch at school with Jennifer and we'd talked about Lisa. Jennifer says her mother keeps trying to protect her from knowing anything more about it, but of course every so often there's some-thing in the paper. She said one day the police came by (a dectective who'd been at the house once before), and they showed her a copy of a poem Lisa wrote about reading poetry with a boy. No, talking about poetry to him. They wanted to know if Lisa had told her anything about him. Jennifer said she thought the poem was just made up—

what Lisa wished would happen. Anyway, when her mother came home, Jennifer said she was furious and told her if any detectives ever came again when she was out, Jennie was to tell them she isn't allowed to talk with them.

Jennifer is really missing Lisa, I can see.

Anyway, when I got home from school I went out to the kitchen to get something to eat and the phone rang. It was HIM. He said he was calling my mother, but when he found I was home alone, he said he was leaving work early and would I like to go for a walk. (I had just told him I was feeling sad about Lisa.) So I left a note for my mother, saying I was going for a walk (I didn't tell her with anybody), and I met him where we said and we walked all around campus. There are neat paths there that I didn't even know about. We talked about school and his work and I came home feeling so good. He said maybe my mother wouldn't understand about our being together (that's the way he said it: our being together), but I told him I hadn't mentioned that we had tea together or that we were going for a walk. He said maybe that was best, that it should be our little secret. He smiled when he said it. He has the most adorable smile. Like Daddy's. He sort of twinkles. He asked me to meet him again tomorrow, but I'm going with my class to San Francisco to an art museum, so he said he'd call me.

I know it's silly with a grown-up man who thinks I'm just a kid, but I'M IN LOVE!

Sean better not find this. He hasn't come near me since that time. I think he's afraid I will tell Mother how awful he is.

Oh, I hear her coming in the front door. I'm going to put this away.

She did.

26

"She went to a movie. By herself," Libby said. The children were in bed and, for a wonder, Kurt had come home at what she considered a normal time.

"She did? Anything on TV?" he said.

"You don't seem to realize how unusual that is."

"Your mother's going to a movie? What's so unusual about it?"

"I've told you; she never goes out at night. Not alone. You know, Kurt, I'm worried about her."

"Why?" He turned over the newspapers that lay on the coffee table. "Where the hell's the *TV Guide*?"

"Oh, damn it, listen to me for two minutes, will you? TV can wait. I tell you I'm worried about her. I've never seen her so depressed. Never."

Kurt gave up his search and settled back on the couch. "That murder?"

"Yes, she's going through it all again, reliving what happened to her friend's daughter. You know, I don't think anyone realizes what a—toll that sort of thing takes. Here it is fourteen years later and everything's as vivid as though it were yesterday."

"Mmm." Kurt was looking at her absently.

"Kurt, what's wrong?"

"Wrong?"

"Yes, wrong. Lately you just aren't here. Either you really aren't—you're at work or someplace—or you're a million miles away mentally."

He gave an impatient gesture. "That's crap. You've just taken to nagging, something I thought you'd never do. I didn't think you were *capable* of it."

"It's not nagging, Kurt. It's wanting to know what's going on." She considered for a moment. "Kurt, are you having an affair?"

He laughed shortly. "When exactly would I have time for an affair?"

"Evenings. You're out often enough. And sometimes you don't seem to be at work in the daytime."

"Is this the business of that phone call you made when they couldn't find me?"

"That and other things. Kurt, *are* you having an affair?"

"Jesus!" He picked up a pillow and threw it across the room. It barely missed a pottery bowl Libby particularly cherished. "You *are* nagging; I don't care what you call it. What do you expect of me? We weren't married last week, after all. A certain amount of routine settles in."

"Or ennui?"

"Boredom with this topic, certainly."

She decided to risk the whole game. "It isn't just that. Do you realize you've made love to me twice in over five weeks? Is that usual for a couple married seven years?"

"You knew when you married me that I wasn't a twenty-year-old stud."

"That's nonsense. You aren't so old you should be bowing out of sex altogether. I think it's going someplace else."

"My affair?"

"Yes, your affair." She looked at him levelly. "I saw you with a woman on Ash Street a couple of weeks ago. You went into an apartment house with her and hadn't come out an hour later."

He turned an outraged face to her. "You *spied* on me?"

"Not spied. I happened to be going past and I saw you. I stopped the car; I thought you'd be right out. You know, the funny thing—the sad thing, really—was that I had this sort of excited feeling. I thought, Oh, that's Kurt, in a really delighted way. I do that when I run into you unexpectedly. You can imagine how I felt when you stayed and stayed with that woman."

"For Christ's sake, that was Nora Crane. She works for the magazine. We were going over some things. It isn't an affair."

"Why weren't you going over them in your office? Or hers? Why did you have to go to her apartment to go over them?"

"I don't remember; her kid was coming home early or something. She was leaving for the day, and I said I'd come along and we could finish up."

"When I asked you, you lied to me."

"I didn't lie to you. I just didn't remember. It wasn't anything to remember."

"You remember now."

"Well, of course, you reminded me. Libby, what is it with this jealous wife bit?"

"It's that I want a husband. If I don't have one, I want to know it." She glared at him. "I'm too young to spend my life sitting around waiting for you to deign to give me time. I need a sex life. I need companionship. I need the things I got married for. Among them, a father who's here when his kids are awake."

That cut to the quick. "You can't say I'm not a good father."

"You're a good one when you're here. Half the time the kids go to sleep without seeing you. Now tell me what's going on—I need to know, Kurt." The anger had gone out of her voice. "Just tell me."

He was silent for a moment. "There isn't anything to tell. I'm sorry about the sex. I've been tired and tense. The new plan for the magazine, other things. I just haven't felt very—romantic."

"Why did it take you till now to tell me? Why let me go week

116

after week wondering if we're ever going to sleep together again? Maybe you were trying to—"

He broke in contemptuously. "Drive you into another man's arms?"

"You may sneer, but the thought has occurred to me."

"And whose arms would that be? Robert Carter's?"

"Robert? Why on earth would you think that?"

"You seemed very interested."

"I barely know the man."

"You tell me you paid him a visit the other night."

"That was when I was looking for my mother. For God's sake, what do you expect of me? That I'll sit here alone night after night, watching TV, while you supposedly work?"

"I don't supposedly work. I work."

"Well, whatever. My God, I'd never have thought you'd be jealous of Robert. Your own employee. Maybe Mother was right."

He looked up sharply. "Right about what?"

"I told her about seeing you on Ash Street. She said maybe you were trying to make me jealous, to keep me in line because I was young and you were scared you'd lose me."

Kurt stood up and began to pace the floor. "Jesus Christ, you've talked to your mother about this? What the fuck purpose could that serve? You have no judgment at all."

"I was upset. I needed to talk to someone. What's wrong with my telling my mother?"

"Not a thing!" He came to a stop before her. "Not a frigging thing except that for the rest of our lives together, I'll be uncomfortable, with her thinking I'm a philanderer of some sort. You've effectively ruined my relationship with Alicia, that's all."

"Well, I'm sorry. It was more important that I talk with someone than that I worry about your relationship with my mother."

"And with whom else have you shared our little secret? I suppose you discussed our sex life with Ruth as well?"

"As a matter of fact, I did. But I haven't talked with anyone

117

else." Except Robert, she thought. But I'd better not tell him that.

"That does it. I'm getting the hell out of here before I say something I really regret."

Suddenly her anger was at white heat. "If you go, you'd better not come back."

"Maybe I won't." He picked up his jacket form the chair. "Maybe I just fucking won't."

27

Meredith came home from San Francisco late and more tired than she had expected to be. No one was at home to greet her. Her mother had left a note, telling her to open a can of soup for supper and that she wouldn't be back late.

The day had been fun, despite having to pass up the walk with HIM. On the bus she had sat next to a boy in her class whom she had never before noticed; they had talked steadily all the way to San Francisco, although now she couldn't remember exactly what they had talked about.

She dumped a can of tomato soup into a pan and heated it, remembering to keep the gas turned low and to stir, and then she ate it standing at the stove. When she had finished, she went into her room to get into her pajamas and housecoat. It was good that Sean wasn't home; she felt uneasy in the house alone with him. Once more she wondered if she should talk to her mother. Probably not. It was no big thing, just Sean-craziness.

As she undressed, she considered. Should she bother to

write tonight? Maybe just a few words; after all, that had been a pretty special exhibit, and she didn't want her journal to be only about her feelings. She opened the hamper and dragged out the journal.

Saturday, April 9

The Impressionist exhibit was interesting. It wasn't exactly what I expected, but it was very surprising the way people who saw the Impressionists' paintings when they first made them thought about them. There were little clippings from magazines that came out at that time and then quotations from things people say now. One man wrote that in a painting by Renoir, the woman had green skin that looked as if it was decaying. It looked lovely to me, as though you'd like to touch the woman in the painting, but when I squinted I could see there really was green in places. Funny.

On the way in I sat next to a boy in my class. He's more comfortable to talk to than most boys, almost like a girl friend. He waited for me and we rode back together, too. But I kept comparing him with HIM and thinking how different a grown man is, so much more—what's the word I mean? Sophisticated, I guess. Like he knows what the world is about. I learned a new word the other day: callow. *I kept thinking that boy seemed callow next to HIM. My mother always says comparisons are odious, whatever that means. It means you shouldn't compare people, I guess, but it's hard not to.*

I was thinking. I wonder what I'd paint if I were making an impression of HIM. Mostly dark hair and a smile, I think. The smile would be pretty big—I didn't pay attention to whether the Impressionists made the important things bigger than the unimportant ones. If they do, he'd be almost nothing but smile.

If I were doing one of me, I guess I'd make sort of a stick figure with red hair. I feel like a stick figure, especially tonight. Some of the kids in my class diet all the time— they hardly eat anything they're so worried about being fat. I envy them. I'd give anything to have some womanly curves. Even my mother, who is a woman, doesn't have womanly curves. I suppose it runs in the family or something.

But it doesn't seem to matter to HIM. After I wrote that, I almost crossed it out, but I promised myself I wouldn't cross anything in this journal out. But I make it sound like he's my boyfriend, and I know better than that, at least I think I do. I certainly have mixed-up feelings about him. Sometimes all I want is for him to be like a father. Other times I get all sloppy as though I'm IN LOVE with him. I wish Lisa was still here. I could tell her about it and she'd understand. Jennie's sort of more grown-up—I always feel a little childish around her, and though I can tell her some things, I couldn't tell her about these feelings.

I'm really too tired to write tonight. I'm going to admit it and stop. ✳

She put the book back in the hamper and unlocked her door; she had pushed the button that locked it. Her mother didn't like her to lock her door, but with Sean acting the way he was, she was going to just the same. But her mother should be home soon.

She yawned and reached for her book. Time to get into bed for a read. If she wasn't too sleepy.

28

The Sunday phone call from Syd Pagano was unexpected; Libby had put him out of her mind after the abortive visit they had with the Bruces. "Kurt in?"

He was in that morning, for a wonder. She called him.

"Syd? What's up? You did? Maybe we'd better go over it. Hang on a second." He turned to Libby. "Here?" he silently mouthed.

She shrugged her acquiescence.

"Yeah, Syd. We're not doing anything special around here. Come on over. The kids are off on a picnic with some friends—it's quiet and we can break out a couple of beers."

Syd arrived almost immediately. God, he's handsome, Libby thought, letting him in. It's enough to make a woman drool. "Come out to the backyard. Kurt's on the patio. When you're done with your business, tell Kurt to give a yell and I'll join you."

Later, sitting with them over a beer, she studied Syd. The way he reacted to things was unusual. He was so taciturn, so noncommital, no matter what was asked or said. Like the Lisa business.

She asked him about it. "Syd, you met that little girl who was killed, didn't you?"

His face stiffened. "For a minute. Kurt was there."

"Libby." Kurt was on his third beer and was feeling expansive. "Let's not discuss that. There are lots of other topics of conversation."

"How's her mother doing?" Libby persisted.

"She's back. She's all right," Kurt said.

"Is she really—functioning?" Libby asked. "Really working?"

"She's doing *fine*," Kurt said.

"Maybe overreacting a little," Syd put in.

"My God." Libby was indignant. "How can you overreact to something like that?" she began, but Kurt cut her off.

"Let's not discuss it. If you don't mind, Libby."

"It's just—" She appealed to Syd. "Do you find it as difficult to talk about as Kurt does?" she said. "I hear the police came and interviewed all of you, asked if the girls had told you anything." Suddenly she remembered. "The other one was that little Crane girl?"

"Yes," said Kurt, his mouth a thin line.

"Do you find it so hard to discuss, Syd?" The beer must be getting to her, she was being so insistent.

His already dark face flushed. "Yes, I do." He pushed back his chair. "You know, I really should be pushing off."

Libby was abject. "Don't go, Syd. I'm sorry; of course it must upset you both working with Lisa's mother like that. We don't have to talk about it."

"I told you," Kurt said.

She glared at him. "As a mother, I have a right to be concerned."

"To be concerned, yes, but not to dwell full time on it."

"Full time! I don't—"

"I really do have to go." Syd was on his feet. "Good-bye Libby. It was good seeing you."

Kurt walked with him to the door. She stayed on the patio, tilting her glass against the sun and finally downing the rest of the beer in one long gulp.

"Jesus," her husband said when he returned. "You just don't have any sense at all, do you?"

Apparently not the right sort for you and your friends, she thought, staring sullenly back at him. I don't seem to please you in any respect these days.

L ater, Syd phoned. Kurt had gone to pick up the children.

"Libby, I behaved badly earlier at your house. I want to apologize."

Libby was at a loss for words. Most people would have let it go, not referred to it again. "That's all right, Syd," she said, trying for lightness. "Don't think twice about it. I shouldn't—I shouldn't talk about it. It's just so much on my mind."

"I know. It was"—there was a long pause—" a terrible thing."

"Mostly it's my mother," Libby said. Somehow she was unable to leave the subject alone. "She had a friend several years ago who had this happen to her."

"To her? To her child, you mean?"

"Yes. Mother's been reexperiencing the whole thing. It's beginning to affect me—her depression."

"I can understand that."

There was an uncomfortable silence. Libby could think of nothing to say.

"At any rate," Syd went on," I do apologize."

"You mustn't, Syd. It was my fault. Come to dinner one day soon. I promise I won't bring up a word about Lisa Margolin."

"Thank you, I'd like to."

Damn it, she thought, he's just making polite, empty sounds. "How about—say, a week from Friday?" she said, calling his bluff.

"A week from Friday? Well . . . that'll be fine." He sounded resigned, but she was unrelenting.

"Let's make it latish—eight? Then the kids'll be down for the night."

"Fine. See you then."

Now, she thought as she hung up, what did I do that for? And what's Kurt going to think?

29

Meredith sighed and yawned and then headed for the hamper. She was sleepy but she wanted to write. She wasn't sure why. She was troubled by something she couldn't name.

Unearthing the red journal from beneath the soiled clothing, she sat down at her desk. For a moment she went blank, unsure of what she wanted to write. Then she picked up her pen.

Wednesday, April 13

I've been thinking about Lisa all day. Funny, at times I just seem to forget. In fact, the other day I reached for the telephone, thinking, Lisa will know about that, I'll call her. And it was as though I'd burned my hand on the receiver—I jumped away and thought, But she's dead, Lisa's dead. She was too young to die. All the things she was going to do.

Today it's twenty-four days since Lisa was discovered, and the police haven't found out anything. And five since

*I heard from HIM. I keep thinking maybe I acted too
dumb, too young last time we were together. Or maybe he
was mad because I couldn't go walking with him Saturday. I thought at least he'd call me, maybe not to suggest a
walk like last time, but to ask me to have iced tea again or
something. It's stupid. I'm stupid. I act as if he's my
boyfriend or something. I don't know what's the matter
with me.*

Meredith threw down her pen and scrubbed her hand across
her eyes. What was she crying about, for Pete's sake? She really
must think he was her boyfriend. Anybody could tell she was
crazy. She picked up the pen again.

*One other thing. About Sean. Something funny happened.
I was walking down on the mall the other day, and I
thought I saw someone familiar. Then he disappeared.
Then I saw him again and he saw me look and ducked
into a store. When I walked back to the store, he was gone.
It was as though Sean was following me. I suppose it was
just coincidence. He probably didn't want me to talk to
him or walk with him and he ducked out of sight. It gave
me a funny feeling, but I'm sure it was nothing.*

She could think of nothing else to write. Her mind was
empty, except for this terrible anxiety that she had done
something dumb and spoiled everything with HIM.

30

"Of course he came back." Ruth held the skirt she was hemming away from her. "Is that straight?"

"What? Oh. It looks all right to me. Yes, he came back. Late, though. I couldn't help wondering where he was."

"Probably at the magazine. You really think he has someone?"

"I do, Ruth. And I don't know what to do about it. I don't want to bring up my kids by myself. Besides, he adores them; he'd never give them up without a fight."

"Hey, wait a minute." Ruth put down her sewing. "You're jumping the gun. You're not going to leave Kurt, not without some proof and not without some discussion. You have to find out what's what."

"But he denies it all. Says he went to what's-her-name's—Nora Crane's—place to work that day I saw him."

"Maybe you need to talk to her."

"I don't know the woman. Oh, I guess I've met her—pretty,

with dark hair, about Kurt's age. But I don't really know her. What could I say: have you been sleeping with my husband?"

"Why not? That's the question, isn't it?"

"Oh, Ruth, you know damned well *you* wouldn't do that. You suggest such forthright measures, but in fact you'd never carry them out if it were you."

"I don't know. I might. Especially if something so important to me were at stake. You could go to her and in best I-message fashion tell her you've been worried, perhaps needlessly, and so on. Not accuse her or anything."

"Eye message? What are you talking about?"

"Didn't you ever read about Parent Effectiveness Training? The idea is to say what *you* feel—I feel this—rather than accuse the kid of being no damned good."

"Oh. I guess I've heard of it. But who remembers that sort of thing? When you're mad you don't choose your words."

"Well, you can this time. You can plan what you'll say and just how you'll say it. You can't come out of it any worse off than you are now, talking about leaving Kurt on the basis of a suspicion."

"You know, Kurt was furious when I told him I'd talked to Mother and you about this. That was what really sent him out of the house last night."

"If there's no validity to your accusations, naturally he'd be furious. He'd feel as though from now on we'll be expecting him to go astray, do you dirt."

Libby leaned back in her chair, looking at the ceiling. "Shit. I don't know *what* to do." She sighed deeply.

"Go see Nora Crane. It's simple, it's direct."

"I—I'll think about it. What if I ran into Kurt there? Would I-messages be of any use then?"

"Don't sneer at them, they work. Go when you know Kurt's at home. Make up an excuse to get out and leave him with the kids."

Libby looked at her friend with appreciation. "You've really got this figured. You're good."

"Well"—Ruth bit off the thread and put down the skirt—" as you point out, maybe I'm better when it's someone else's problem. But go see her, Lib. It may be the only way you'll find out."

K urt arrived home for dinner at six. He was sullen but he said nothing about going back to the magazine after dinner. When he volunteered out of turn to bed the children down, Libby made her move. "Mother seems worried about something, Kurt. As long as you're putting the kids down, I'm going to run out," No mention had been made of the evening before.

"How late will you be?"

"Not late. I'll just run over and back." She thought, now I'll have to stop at Mother's for a minute, in case he calls or something is said.

When she got out to the car, she found she was trembling. Trying to get hold of herself, she flooded the engine and reflooded it before she could start the car. As she rounded the corner, she realized she was taking a roundabout route. "Jesus, Libby," she said aloud, "get control of yourself!"

When, finally, she pulled her car up before the apartment house on Ash, she had to sit for a moment. "I-messages," she said aloud and then got out of the car and entered the building. Crane was apartment 5. For a panicky moment she hoped Nora Crane would be out, but immediately a voice came over the intercom.

"It's Libby Altman. Kurt's wife."

There was a moment's silence, then the voice spoke again. "Come on up. I'll buzz."

By the time she reached the apartment, Libby had stopped trembling. She felt remote, distant, in command of herself. Cool. And a little unreal. The door was open; in it stood a petite dark-haired woman who wore no makeup. The scarlet of her housecoat was too strong a color for her pale skin. She was, Libby noted coldly, the complete opposite of her leggy blonde self.

"I'm sorry, I've gotten comfortable already," Nora Crane said, indicating the housecoat. "Is something wrong? Kurt's not sick?"

"No, I just wanted to talk with you."

Apprehension touched the woman's face and was gone. "Come in. We can go in here. The kids are busy—Meredith, that's my daughter—is doing her homework and my son's out running an errand." She led Libby into the book-lined room.

"I came," Libby said, sitting down without removing her jacket, "because I've been feeling anxious."

"Anxious?"

"Yes, worried. Kurt's been away from the house a great deal, and I saw him coming in here with you one day. . . ." I-messages, she reminded herself, how the hell do you do them? "It made me apprehensive. Uncomfortable. I need to ask if there's anything between Kurt and you, for my own"—sanity, she thought, but said—"peace of mind."

Nora Crane sat silent, as though thinking how to answer.

"Just tell me the truth. It'll be better all around."

"The truth might confuse you. Kurt does spend a lot of time here," Nora Crane said.

"Then you're—"

"No, we aren't. That's why I said it might confuse you. He—I live here alone with the kids. I'm divorced, and I get hungry for male company. Actually the first time Kurt came here, he came to work with me on something. Then we got to talking and I told him how worried I am over Sean—he's my teenager and is driving me up the wall—and Kurt said he'd be glad to get acquainted with Sean and see if he could help. It's because Sean has no men in his life that he's the way he is, I'm sure of it."

"His father doesn't—"

"His father doesn't *anything*. And Sean's into drugs. I know he is, maybe only pot, I pray it's only pot, but he isn't himself a lot of the time."

"And Kurt came to visit him?"

"Yes, at first. Actually he could never get Sean to warm up to him, and to tell the truth I don't think he likes Sean, either. But he's continued to come."

130

"Just to *visit*?"

"Yes." Nora looked down at her hands. "I'll tell you the truth, Mrs. Altman—"

"Libby."

"Libby. I wouldn't have said no if something had developed. I figured if there weren't trouble at home, he wouldn't be here at all, so I wasn't doing anything to undermine his marriage. But"—she turned her hands palms up and looked directly at Libby—"there's been nothing. Not the suggestion of a pass. Frankly I don't understand it myself."

"He likes kids," Libby said. "He probably really wanted to help with your son." The statement sounded lame.

"I know, but that doesn't really explain it. Or maybe it does. Are things going wrong between you two?"

Libby thought of the infrequency with which Kurt turned to her in bed these days. "No," she said. "Not exactly."

"Which means yes."

"No. Kurt has seemed a little cool to me"—Why am I telling her this? Libby wondered—"but otherwise things have been as usual. I've heard the seventh year of a marriage is a tough one."

"It was the eleventh for me. But that was after ten years of not getting along. To put it politely." She sounded bitter.

"Have you ever asked Kurt why he comes here so frequently?"

"And kill the goose that lays the golden eggs? I prefer having him here to not having him here, whatever his reason. Maybe I won't after this conversation, but I did till now."

"I don't understand." Libby looked at the other woman with curiosity. She found she was beginning to like her. "You're attractive. There must be dozens of men—"

"Don't kid yourself. You hold on to Kurt. These days, especially after you hit forty, it isn't easy. Oh, I have little flings now and then with what's out there, but they aren't Kurts, any of them."

"What do you think I should do? Tell Kurt I came to see you? You won't call him, will you?" she asked, with sudden anxiety.

"I won't tell him—I won't call him, at least—I'll give you a chance to talk to him first. And I must say I've begun to feel quite platonic where he's concerned, so it'll be no great loss to me if he sticks to our professional relationship in the future. But I do think you should find out what's wrong between you two. That must be at the bottom of it."

Libby sighed. "I guess." She stood up. "I have to get back. Please don't call Kurt. That is,"—she remembered—"I'd like you not to call."

"I won't. I said I wouldn't." She rose, too.

"You're—I'm glad you were honest with me." Were you? she wondered. "I can see why Kurt likes you."

"Well,"—the other woman laughed without amusement—"coming from you, that's something. Oh, Meredith,"—her daughter had entered the living room—"this is Mr. Altman's wife. You know him—Kurt."

Meredith politely extended a hand.

Libby looked at her. She was very like her mother, with the incipient loveliness of her mother, but red haired, not dark. A mature-seeming twelve-year-old despite her little-girl looks. Libby smiled. "I'm pleased to meet you, Meredith."

Meredith looked puzzled. "Is Kurt all right? You aren't here because he's sick or something?"

"No, Mrs. Altman and I had some things to discuss. Run along, Meredith, I want to say good-bye to my guest." Her tone was firm.

After the bedroom door had closed on Meredith, Nora said, "I'm sure she's confused by this visit. She probably assumed that Kurt was unattached, one of what she calls my boyfriends. She'll be out here asking questions after you go."

"Adult carryings on are enough to confuse the young." Libby followed Meredith's example and extended her hand. "Thank you. I'll talk with Kurt."

As she walked down the hall to the elevator, she thought, Strange. What has Kurt been getting from her that I'm not giving him? She did not look forward to the conversation with him.

En route home, she stopped at her mother's, although subterfuge was no longer necessary. Again the house was dark. What's going on, she thought, what is all this going out at night? Does she have a *man*? On impulse she pulled the car up and ran up the path to Robert's.

After a moment he opened the door. He looked sleepy.

"I'm sorry. I seem to do this all the time, but have you any idea where my mother is?"

He looked at her blankly and then laughed. "I was asleep, must have dozed off over my book. No. If you were the mother and she the daughter, I'd understand all this concern. I do think your mother's grown-up enough to go out at night." His eyes were amused.

Libby felt sudden confusion. "I know. I must sound like an idiot. No, I won't come in"—he had stepped back and waved a hand—"and I'm sorry I interrupted your nap. It's just that Mother never goes out at night, and twice now I've come by and not found her in. I think"—she tried for a light laugh—"she must be leading a double life."

"Well, I don't know about that, but I didn't see her leave and I have no idea where she is. You're sure you won't come in?"

"No." She started to back away, aware that overwhelmingly she wanted to enter the warm room beyond. "My husband's baby-sitting. I have to get back."

Driving home, she thought, Here I am questioning Kurt's motives and I find myself drawn to another man. Maybe Kurt's just resisting temptation the way I am. The thought did not make her feel better.

31

In her journal Meredith wrote:

Thursday, April 14

*Well, talk about weird! Kurt has a wife. Just now I went
into the living room and there they sat, my mother and
his wife, lovey-dovey as could be. Wait till I tell Jennie! In
fact, I think maybe I'll tell Jennie everything—I don't
know. I have to think about it. He said it should be our
secret.*

*Nothing much has happened since I wrote the last time. I
haven't seen HIM (I almost said his name, wrote it, I
mean. I'd better not get careless, that crazy brother of
mine would tell Mother for sure). HE's funny. He seems to
like me but—well, the feeling I have is that he's afraid of
me. I can't imagine what there is to be afraid of, but when
we were on our walk I'd catch him looking at me in the
strangest way, and the only word I can think of to describe*

it is afraid. *Maybe he's afraid he's falling in love with me, ha ha.*

He told me a lot about himself while we walked and he asked about me. I told him how weird Sean is (I didn't tell him details) and how sometimes I'm almost afraid to be alone with him. He said I shouldn't, then—be alone with Sean, I mean. He said girls can't always trust boys and men. Of course I know that, but I don't really think Sean would do anything bad to me. He is my brother, after all.

He told me about when he grew up. He had a strange mother, he said. She scared him although she didn't do anything to him. He said his father sort of wasn't there. He was a salesman and was away a lot and when he was home didn't spend any time with him. It made me feel sad. I don't have a father, either, but when you come right down to it, my mother is pretty nice. She doesn't scare me, that's for sure. Sometimes I feel sorry for her, though. She seems to choose the wrong men for herself. I hope I don't do that when I grow up. What I'd like is to marry someone just like HIM.

In the other part of the house, Meredith heard the door close. She waited what seemed an appropriate length of time and then went out, looking as casual as possible.

Her mother was curled into a corner of the leather couch, staring into space. "I expected you'd show up," she said to Meredith.

"I didn't know Kurt had a wife," Meredith said.

"Well, now you know."

"Why did she come here?"

Her mother made an irritable little motion with one hand. "She was checking up on him. Really, Meredith, this is none of your affair."

"But—are you wrecking their marriage?"

Her mother looked up. "Where did you get that—wrecking their marriage? Honestly, Meredith, sometimes one would think your major reading was the *National Enquirer* or the *Star*. You don't read those rags, do you? Let me catch you spending your allowance on—"

"Don't worry, I don't." Sometimes her mother was dumb. "I just meant if he's married, what's he doing messing around with other—women? He is your boyfriend, after all."

"He isn't my boyfriend. He's a friend. I don't know what you think we do together. All we do is talk."

"Well—"

"Well what?"

"With the others—"

"Meredith, you sound as though I had streams of men passing through. There've only been a couple of others. You know, Meredith, you'd do better to pay attention to your own affairs. Have you finished your homework?"

Meredith set her mouth. "Yes," she said. Treating her as a baby as usual. If she told her mother what she really did and who she was friends with, she'd see she was more grown-up than she thought. She considered doing that and abandoned the idea. "Anyway," she said, "if his wife was checking up on him, she must *think* he's doing something he shouldn't be."

"I don't give a damn what she thinks." Her mother leaned forward and reached for the cigarette box.

"I thought you weren't—"

"Now, Meredith." Her mother's eyes narrowed. "I don't need a lecture on smoking. Or on my social conduct. You go into your room and write in your diary or something." She lit a cigarette and took a drag on it. "*Now.*"

Back in her bedroom, Meredith eyed the journal. Being instructed to write in it had destroyed her desire to share with it the conversation she had just had with her mother. She looked at what she had written and finished it off.

One of the things about HIM is that he makes me feel the way my father used to—sort of taken care of and paid attention to. I always wish I could say to my father, "Daddy, why don't you at least visit me? Don't you love me anymore?" But I can't. When I'm around him, I feel tongue-tied, sort of as though I'm frozen. And I don't see him that much, anyway. I don't understand it. He must have changed as much as Sean has.

She couldn't put the book away without comment on her mother's and her conversation. She added a line.

My mother is impossible. Impossible!

She tucked the journal back into its hamper hiding place and picked up her book.

32

Libby settled herself before the phone and prepared to listen to Ruth. It was Joel again. The third turndown that week had soured him. He was not interested in anybody or anything but that damned film.

"What a grouch," Ruth said. "I just called to ask if he wanted to eat in or out." Then, her voice changed, she added, "Lib, if he doesn't make it with this film, he says he's going to have to find something else—out of the Bay Area. What will happen to us then?"

"Maybe—"

"He hasn't heard from Docufilm. I keep thinking maybe that'll be good news. It would mean not only distribution but cassettes, everything."

"We'll just have to keep our fingers crossed. Maybe they'll take it. They just have to."

"The trouble is, Libby, that they don't have to. The strike has slowed things down. They may be in need of a finished film or two, but believe me, they don't have to take it."

138

"From your point of view, they have to."

"Oh, from our point of view." Her voice softened. "Finally, he simmered down. He'd dumped his problems on someone else. He's going to let *me* do the worrying." She laughed. "One thing, Lib, I let it slip out that you'd gone to see Nora Crane."

"Oh." Why did she tell everything to Ruth? She knew everything went straight to Joel. Well, what the hell. The idea was Ruth's in the first place. "It's all right," she said. "What was his reaction?"

"Just that when you told Kurt he'd be furious."

"That's all?"

"No. He was interested that Mrs. Crane was worried about her children."

"Not about her daughter. Her son."

"Well, I guess I said the daughter, too. He met the daughter, you know."

"He did?"

"When her mother and Mrs. Margolin took the girls to the magazine."

"Oh, that time. Kurt told me about that."

"Joel said the girl seemed like a perfectly ordinary twelve-year-old. He couldn't see what she was worried about."

"It was her *son*. His name is Sean."

"Anyway. I told Joel he acts as though he has a *Heaven's Gate* on hands. Talk about grandiose notions. He did laugh when I said that. Can you imagine what it feels like to spend *millions* and then have a film flop? It must be awful."

"Cheer up, Ruth. *Bible Story* is just on the verge of being discovered. I can feel it in my bones."

Ruth laughed. It was not a happy sound.

J ust before dinner Kurt called, coldly announcing that he'd be late, very late. He's showing me, she thought. Nobody's going to own Kurt Altman; he's his own man.

At least, she told herself, *I* told him; Nora Crane didn't. She found some small triumph in that. The situation on the whole was mystifying. She couldn't explain it, couldn't recall any alteration in her relationship with her husband, except for the sex. When had that started? Or rather, she reflected with some bitterness, when had that stopped? Had she said or done something? She rummaged back through the past weeks. Except for his absences in the evening, Kurt had seemed the same. She couldn't recall any particular quarrel or disagreement that might have set him off. Several weeks earlier they had talked about redoing the kitchen and he had flatly refused, saying they could barely afford the house, much less a new kitchen, but that couldn't have been it—she wasn't a demanding wife. Maybe—she edged away from the idea and then returned to it—he did lust after Nora Crane, but was showing restraint. No chance. In another mood, she would have laughed at the idea. Kurt wasn't the sort to sacrifice himself easily. Such behavior would be totally uncharacteristic. But the thought depressed her; she put it out of her mind.

Wednesday night, after she had told him about her visit to Nora Crane, she had tried to talk to him about it, but he had been so angry she had given up. She had also tried to persuade him to a commitment to stay away from Nora Crane's, but that too had been impossible. She wondered glumly if she had done irrevocable damage to their marriage with her interference. But was it interference? Hadn't she a right, a claim on Kurt and his time? I could do the same as he does, she thought, I could drop in on some man, say Robert, this evening. How would Kurt like that?

Or I could ask him to come by for a drink. He'd come in a minute. The idea reinforced her sense of herself of as a desirable woman. *He* likes me, she thought. If Kurt weren't his boss he'd probably go to bed with me in a flash.

She picked up the phone, then put it down. But her anger was out of control. After calling information for Robert's number—which was probably right there in Kurt's address file, but she'd be damned if she'd look—she dialed his number.

He picked up the phone after the first ring.

"Robert." Suddenly her face was hot. She was making all

sorts of unwarranted assumptions. Now she had to say something. "I—my wandering husband is out again tonight. I thought
maybe you'd like to come by to keep me company. I baked a
chocolate cake today." God, she thought, chocolate cake. What
have I sunk to?

"Well"—there was a long moment of hesitation—"do you
think Kurt would like that?"

Fuck what Kurt would like, she thought in sudden fury.
"Probably not." Obviously he was far more interested in his job
than in her. "Don't, if you feel it'd jeopardize—"

"Why don't you come here? Can you get a sitter?"

"What? Oh, I guess—I think I can." But she was uncomfortable with the invitation. "Don't feel you have to ask me. I
just—well, I was feeling alone and I thought you might—"

"I don't feel I have to. It just seems more sensible"—read
discreet, she edited—"to be here. I have a good bottle of wine,
and I've been waiting for a special occasion to open it. A
sufficiently special occasion." He spoke gently. She wasn't sure
whether he was being kind or ardent. She wondered what she
had gotten herself into.

What the hell, whatever it was, she could cope. "I'll check
with the sitter and ring you right back." She hung up with a
little flourish; she was excited. Was it at seeing Robert? Or at
getting even with Kurt? Or just, she giggled as she thought
about it, just at getting the hell out of the house for an evening
for a change?

Her mother's windows were bright with light. When I
want her to be in, she's out; when I want her to be out, she's in;
that's mothers for you, Libby thought as she slid the car past
her mother's place and parked down around the turn in the
road. God, she thought, I'm acting as guilty as a kid who's
sneaked out of the house. Is that the way Kurt affects me? Or
is it Robert?

Carter took both her hands and drew her into the house. He

held them for a moment. "This is a very nice alteration of my plans for the evening," he said, smiling. "I had thought I'd go over some layouts, and I was mightily resisting getting started."

She withdrew her hands and removed her jacket, seating herself across the room from him. "Tonight Mother's home," she said. "Wouldn't you know?" And then, "You must think I'm pretty odd, calling you out of the blue when we're barely acquainted."

He grinned. "Not odd. Delightful. I think people should be spontaneous. We enjoyed each other the other evening; why shouldn't I come to mind when you're feeling lonely?"

She looked away from him. "It's not lonely exactly. It's—I guess I should be honest. Kurt and I are having some trouble. Over another woman."

"And you're getting even?"

She was shocked, she wasn't sure whether because the idea was repugnant to her or because it was so accurate. "No!" she said. "Not getting even. Just not sitting around waiting for him to come home." She looked at him. "You know the woman. Nora Crane."

He studied her face, his own thoughtful. "Nora."

"Yes. What sort of woman is she? Is she honest, do you think?"

"Honest? What do you mean?"

"I went to see her the other night. She said nothing was going on, that Kurt just came to talk about work or her kids. She has a teenage son who's a problem. And a twelve-year-old girl."

"Yes. I met the girl. They—she and her friend came to the magazine for a sort of tour." He was quiet for a moment. "Nora seems like a pretty decent person to me. I think she'd be honest. Of course I haven't been at the magazine as long as some of the others; I don't know her well. Did you believe her?"

"I did. I even liked her—against my better judgment. But I don't understand. If there's nothing going on between them, why is he going there? Doesn't he get enough companionship from me?" Her voice sounded piteous to her; she straightened in the chair and added, "I suppose it's the sameness, the boredom that creeps into every marriage."

142

"Probably. It's probably what brought you here tonight rather than to a woman friend's."

"I suppose." She appealed to him. "What can couples do? They do get bored. These days I know exactly what Kurt's response is going to be to anything I say, and probably he feels the same. But we have something. We have the kids and a lot of shared experience. What do you do, throw all that away? You'd just grow bored with someone else."

He laughed. "It's a problem. Maybe you should come by here and he should visit Nora and that will satisfy both of you."

She smiled, sheepish. "I don't understand people."

"Who does? How about some wine? I tell you this is pretty special stuff; it cost fifteen dollars." He laughed at his own candor. "On my salary that's quite a splash."

She protested. "Don't waste it on me. I'm perfectly happy with three-dollar wine. Two-fifty. Honestly, I don't know the difference."

"No, we'll open this. You'll know the difference. If you don't, I'll instruct you."

The wine was smooth, dry, with an indefinable flavor that made her want more. She did notice the difference. She began to relax.

"Tell me about yourself," he said. That's the beginning, she thought, that's what you always do, tell each other about yourselves, your childhoods, your engaging quirks. Give the other one a glimpse of the edited, idealized image that is the self you offer up to others. But she told him, "You've met Mother. I had a pretty good childhood. Of course my parents were divorced when I was little, and I never saw my father after that. Maybe"—she laughed—"that's why I married a man eighteen years older. But my mother gave me lots of time and made sure things were all right. She was teaching full time, not subbing, and our income was adequate. She had the house then; that was the one thing my father gave her."

"Funny, I hear little sounds of misgiving. It must have been difficult not having a father like the other kids."

"Not so difficult. Even then, divorced parents were common, not as common as they are now—three-quarters of the kids in

143

my daughter's kindergarten class have stepparents or half brothers and sisters or single mothers. What about you?"

He smiled. "Completely ordinary. Two parents. Nothing special."

"You're being evasive. There's something special in every childhood."

"Not mine. Really. More wine? This is good, isn't it? Let me get some crackers and cheese."

While he was in the kitchen, she wandered around the living room. Drawings, books, a shelf of records. He had made the ordinary little mobile home attractive, given it character. It needed something, though; what was it?

He returned with a plate on which a small wedge of Brie was flanked by some crisp crackers. He offered her the plate.

She took a cracker. "I'm looking at your living room. You know, you did something very special here. No one would know it was a mobile home."

"All done on a shoestring."

Color, that was it. It was furnished completely in neutrals. "You could use a bright cushion or two; shall I scout out a couple for you—as gifts from me, I mean, in exchange for listening to my troubles and feeding me your fancy wine?"

He glanced around. "Actually, I like it this way. Backdrop. Let the people provide the color."

She felt faintly chastised, as though her aesthetic judgment had been found wanting. And he probably thought in typical feminine fashion she was taking over. Had she been? She sighed. There were traps everywhere. "Sorry," she said. "I wasn't criticizing. I think it's lovely just as it is. I guess my tastes are more humdrum."

He helped himself to cheese. "Nothing about you is humdrum. I'm just a funny guy, that's all."

The evening slipped by before she realized it. Standing to put on her jacket, feeling somewhat tipsy and slightly panicky at the thought of explanations to Kurt, she considered her host. He was comfortable, easy, and—or was the word *but*?— he had not touched her, not even moved within that distance that suggested intimacy. Only his two hands drawing her in, that was the only moment of closeness.

She looked up at him. "You're a *nice* man," she said. It was an opening, should he choose to take it.

He ducked his head in a mock bow.

"My specialty," he said. "As she walked the few yards to the car, aware of his figure standing in the lighted doorway behind her, she thought, Maybe he has someone. He certainly didn't complicate my life tonight. She wondered if she would have liked it better if he had.

33

Libby was surprised to receive the phone call. Ruth seldom called on the weekend unless the four of them were planning to see each other. Ruth was crying.

"What's the matter, Ruthie?" Ruth crying was alarming.

"It's Joel. I think he's left me. I think I've"—she paused to blow her nose—"driven him away."

"Come on now. What happened? I'm sure you haven't."

"I started in on him—oh, Lib, why do we have such troubles with our relationships?"

Libby considered. "Maybe everyone does."

"Maybe." She sounded doubtful. "What's happening at your end?"

"Kurt wanted to know where I was the other night. I didn't tell him. Did I tell you? I went to Robert Carter's and drank wonderful wine and talked. I told him everything. I guess that wasn't so smart."

"Well, I certainly haven't been smart with Joel. Imagine

starting in on him about why he hasn't married when he's so worried about *Bible Story*."

"That's what you did?"

"Yes. I—suddenly I got curious. After all, he's in his late thirties. Yet he's never once mentioned any other close attachment. It's odd."

"They're all odd. Look at Kurt. Honestly, I think he's *strange*." Ruth laughed. "That's your husband you're talking about."

"In name only, I sometimes think."

"He's out now? You wouldn't be talking—"

"Oh, he's out. I'm tempted to call Nora Crane and tell her to send him home where he belongs. Of course I don't know he's there."

"But you assume."

"Yes. I imagine I've put a crimp in their friendship; he may be going there just to show me. He's still furious with me about everything, telling you and Mother, going to Nora Crane's, even about being out when he came home the other night and then coming in tipsy."

"You came in tipsy?"

"It must have been the cold air. When I got outside Robert's house, suddenly the wine hit me. I barely made it home."

"Do you think Kurt suspected you were there?"

"I don't know. He carefully didn't mention Robert."

"What shall I do, Libby?"

"I don't know. Do you notice we're as dependent on men as though there'd never been a woman's movement?"

"I'm not dependent on Joel. I just love him."

"That's a sort of dependence, love. Not that the women's movement advocates not loving anyone."

"He brought me Peruvian lilies." Her voice was mournful. "He's been talking about how he doesn't earn a decent living, can't give me anything. I'm tempted to call him, but I may mess things up worse. I do dumb things when I'm upset."

"Maybe you'd better wait till you both cool down."

"But I told him if he left not to come back."

There was a silence at the other end of the line. "That was a little foolish. Especially since you didn't mean it."

"You didn't mean it when you said it to Kurt." Ruth began to cry again. "I keep thinking maybe he sort of seized on it, as though maybe he was waiting for a chance to break things off."

"Now why would you think that? It's nonsense."

"I suppose it is. I know he's worried. He thinks *Bible Story* is a lost cause. He's talking about job hunting, that would mean another city. We'd be through for good."

"Why? Why can't you go with him?"

"There's never been any talk about our living together or marrying. I think that's why I raised the issue tonight. Asking him why he's never married—oh shit, I'm a complete fool."

"Come on, you're not. Why don't you come over? I'll pop some corn and we can watch TV, some awful soppy program, and both of us weep to our heart's content over it."

"Joel may—"

"If he calls or comes back, it'll do him good to find that you didn't sit around waiting."

"*Your* new policy."

"That's right. Every time Kurt goes out, I'm going to do something, too. And not say what. Maybe I'll start a mad affair with Robert. Though I notice he's very careful with me."

"He works for Kurt."

"Yes." She sighed. "I'll have to find myself someone who doesn't work for my husband. Come on over, Ruth. Cheer *me* up."

"All right. It'll be a mutual cheer-up. I'll leave now."

Libby hung up and went to the kitchen to get out the popcorn popper. It did seem that everything was in a mess for both of them. Men, she thought, you can't live with them and—well, enough of that. She yanked the popper from the cupboard and set it down with a crack.

34

Meredith reached for the phone. She was deep in a book; the phone's insistence interrupted a passage that had her full attention. Keeping her eyes on the page, she picked up the receiver.

It was HIM. She dropped the book. "Hello," she said. "I thought—I'm glad—I mean it's nice to hear your voice again." She was aware of a sensation of intense relief.

"Nice to hear yours. Mother in? Are you there alone?"

"No. I mean I'm alone. This is my mother's morning to market. I do the laundry," she added and then thought, Dumb, what does he care?

"Up to another stroll? Maybe down by the water this time?"

"I'd *love* to. Though—I have to wait till the wash cycle is finished, till I get the clothes in the dryer. Will that be too late?"

"No. Let's say in an hour? I'll meet you at—how about the lighthouse?"

"Oh, *yes*." She thought, Jeepers, I sound sloppy, as though I'm falling all over him. More soberly, she said, "I'll be there in an hour. It sounds like a nice idea." Why did she keep saying *nice*? "A lovely idea." That was worse.

"Good." He sounded as though he were smiling. "And"—he hesitated—"let's not—let's keep our little secret. Remember?"

"Yes, I remember." She hung up, uneasy. It was fun having secrets from her mother, but his reminders, what seemed like his insistence, on their friendship remaining a secret made her uncomfortable. Probably, she thought in self-reproach, because she wasn't used to keeping things to herself. She had to blab everything, run to her mother with everything. That was probably it.

S he had left a note for her mother—vague, general, not one likely to rouse questions. When she came in, her mother was in the kitchen sitting over a cup of coffee with a magazine.

"Oh, hi," she said. "Did Sean tell you where he was going?"

"No." It seemed to Meredith a hopeful but unrealistic question. Sean never told her where he was going. "Maybe he left a note in his room."

"No. I checked. God, that room is a pigsty. I told him I wasn't going to touch it again, that he'd just have to live in it the way it is until he cleans it up himself."

"But you can't stand it."

Nora smiled faintly. "You know me too well. I'm sitting here resisting the impulse to attack it."

"Maybe he likes it that way."

"No one could like it that way. No one. I wonder where the hell he's taken off for now." She leaned her head against her hand in a weary gesture that touched Meredith.

"Mamma, don't, he's all right." She never called her mother *Mamma* any more.

"Maybe. Meredith, do you know"—she tipped her face up and Meredith saw her cheek was flushed as though she had been crying—"if he's using drugs? Anything besides pot? You can tell me, Meredith."

"I don't know. I've never seen anything. He's out a lot, but he

150

could be—" She couldn't think what he might be doing; she left the sentence unfinished. She put an awkward hand against her mother's shoulder, and for a moment Nora clasped it.

"Where have you been?" her mother asked absently.

"Oh, out walking. By the water. There are a lot of boats out. And surfers—the wind must be right today."

"Mmm. Thanks for doing the laundry. You should fold the things in the dryer."

"I will. It was too nice out to hang around here waiting for them. Will they be all wrinkled?"

"I looked in. Mostly towels and jeans. They'll be okay once you smooth them." She rose tiredly and poured herself another cup of coffee. "You'd think I'd be wired by now, this is my third, but—"

Meredith waited for the *but* that didn't come; then she walked into the utility room to take the things out of the dryer. The high spirits with which she had returned had evaporated. She wished she could tell her mother where she had been and with whom, but she had promised. Besides, her mother was worried enough about Sean without her adding to it. And in her present mood, her mother would reach for anything, anyone to blame—she'd raise the roof.

Slowly she began removing the towels from the dryer.

In her room, she took out her journal. She wanted to record her feelings. This afternoon had been different, although she hadn't quite identified the way in which it had been different. Perhaps if she wrote it down, she'd understand it better.

Saturday, April 16

I went for a walk with HIM today. We walked from the lighthouse—the surfers were swooping, looking like birds on the water—till we came to a little beach, a "pocket beach," he called it. We climbed down and sat on the sand with our backs against the rocks, all alone, and looked at

151

the bay. There was only the sound of the water, and the sailboats were out, little white triangles against the water, and above the sky was bright blue, because the wind was up and all the clouds were blown away. It was so pretty. It made me think of Lisa and her poems.

But I didn't enjoy myself there, exactly. I mean I always like to be with him—he pays so much attention to me, listens to everything I say and thinks it over before he answers. But there was something different about him today. He kept looking at me, then looking away, as though he felt guilty about something. (He reminded me of the way I try to tell whether my mother is mad at me or not. I wasn't mad about anything, so I couldn't understand it.) Then suddenly he got up, like he was upset about something, and walked away from me. After a while he turned around and laughed and said we should go back to the drive.

We walked the rest of the way to the natural bridges at the end and back to the lighthouse. I'd locked my bike there, and he said, "Shall we do it again? How about Tuesday?" and we arranged to meet over in Richards West at about four o'clock. "We have to explore all the natural beauties of the town," he said and sort of twinkled at me. I like him so much when he does that.

The last part of the walk was fun, and we laughed a lot at the pelicans and sea lions and at the surfers tumbling around in the water. I ended up coming home feeling good. I guess I'm too fussy. I want to feel almost like he's my boyfriend, but when he acts like one, I feel funny. I never had a boyfriend and I don't know how you're supposed to act with one.

When I got home my mother was all upset over Sean again. She's afraid he's into crack, too. I can tell. I hope he isn't. He used to be such a nice brother. I don't see how people change like that—sometimes it seems as if he's a completely different person. I wonder if I've changed that much since I was little.

I feel bad, for some reason. Maybe it's my mother worrying about Sean. I don't know. She always says, "Don't *worry, I'll deal with it," about everything, but sometimes I think she can't deal with things at all. I think she needs my father—or someone—as much as I do. I guess I won't write anymore. I want to lie down for a while. I guess I'm tired from the walk.*

It was not accident that Pedersen detoured by way of Cliff Drive. It was the sort of day he loved best—a brisk breeze blowing, the sky clean, the shoreline on the other side of the cove defined sharp as crystal, fearless surfers and scudding sailboats dotting the water. He had stopped on the West Side at a favorite hardware store, big and dim and dusty, to pick up screws for a repair he was doing in his workshop and as usual had spent too much time there; there was something about hardware stores. He came away from the place feeling relaxed and expansive, his parcel (he had bought more than screws) under his arm. Although it might make him late for lunch, he decided to cut around and steal a quick look at the bay en route home.

As he approached the lighthouse, a car pulled out, leaving a parking space. Involuntarily, Pedersen swung in and filled it. Turning off his car's engine, he leaned on the steering wheel, taking in the panorama ahead and below. Spectators clustered against the rail, watching the surfers. A young mother held her wriggling child up to see. A pair of schoolboys pointed out details of surfing style to each other. A couple, ignoring the drama of the scene below, clung together with the urgency of a pair about to be torn apart forever. Across the grass to one side, a girl bent, unlocking her bicycle, her red hair tossed by the wind. Near her, a dark haired figure stood watching, his back to Pedersen—her father, no doubt. Pedersen glanced at them and looked back at the surfers.

Then some familiarity tugged at him. He turned again just as the red-haired youngster mounted her bike, waved a hand and took off. That was Meredith, Lisa's friend; although he had seen her just the once he was sure. He turned and craned to catch a glimpse of the man who had walked away as she left, but he

153

had disappeared, perhaps into the crowd who watched the surfers. Pedersen got out of his car and walked the length of the railing, surveying the group. No familiar dark-haired figure. Damn.

He got back into his car and pulled out, the visit spoiled for him. Meredith Crane had vanished up one of the many small side streets off the drive.

He rode the rest of the way back home thoughtful, unsure how to proceed. If the man was not a relative, was, in fact—he let the idea into his mind—the murderer, he would do well to be careful in how he approached Meredith. Questioning her in front of her mother, for example, might bring complete denial. For that matter, questioning her at all might. He tried to bring back into recollection the appearance, the contours of the man. He was no better than the woman at the swimming pool; all he had registered was hair color: dark.

"What do you think?" he asked Freda over toasted cheese sandwiches.

"You have to be casual."

"That's what I think. Maybe run into her. I could park near the house and appear on the scene as she comes out of her building."

"Yes. Or run into her on school grounds."

"Too iffy. And I'd be too noticeable."

In the end, he parked outside the house that same afternoon, down the street a distance. He felt foolish. Stakeouts weren't his cup of tea, especially stakeouts of children. Besides, for all he knew she was already out of the house somewhere or would emerge with her mother. Or her brother.

As it happened, luck was with him. Within the hour she came running down the steps heading toward him. He got out of his car. "Miss Crane, isn't it? Meredith? I was just coming to see you."

She stopped. "You're the detective who—have you found out something about Lisa?"

"Not yet. Going somewhere?"

"Just to the store."

"Mind if I walk along?" He matched his pace to hers. "You know," he said, "I thought I saw you this morning."

She darted an uneasy glance at him. "You did?"

"I thought so. I was driving along Cliff Drive and the bay was so beautiful I stopped to admire. I thought I saw you getting on your bike." He waited.

She was obviously considering her answer. "I took a bike ride along the drive."

"I thought maybe you walked. Your bike seemed to be locked."

She threw him a suspicious glance. "I walked a little. Did you come to ask me this?"

She was direct; he suppressed a smile. "No, I wanted to check out a couple of things pertaining to Lisa. The dark-haired man she was seen with—have you any notion at all as to who he might have been?"

"No." She seemed to be thinking. "Is that all you know about him, the color of his hair?"

"That's all."

"And he's the one you think killed her?"

"He's the one. It was a good day for a walk on the drive. Did you walk to the bridges?"

"I did today. We—I sat on a little pocket beach and then walked to the natural bridges and back to the lighthouse."

"We?"

"I was with a friend."

"A man, Meredith?"

She stopped and faced him. "You didn't come to talk to me about Lisa."

"You're right. I came to talk to you about you. Meredith, that killer is out there. He likes twelve-year-old girls. Especially, apparently, twelve-year-old girls built like you."

She flushed. "Childish looking?"

"We think so. Probably someone who hasn't yet acquired womanly features is less threatening. I need to know who you were with today, Meredith."

"It was just a friend. He didn't do anything to me."

"Maybe not yet. We don't want him to have the opportunity to do anything to you."

She began walking again, faster now. "I won't go walking with him anymore, but I won't tell you who he was."

"Why not?"

"Because he's not a murderer. He just likes me like an uncle. Or a father. He doesn't go around killing people."

"Do you see your father?"

She didn't answer.

"You don't. And you're hungry for a father. I can understand that. This person might take advantage of your—need."

"I'm not *hungry* for a father." Her young voice had taken on a bitter tone.

"Perhaps not. Meredith, tell me the name of the person you walked with today."

"I won't." She turned her face away; he could see she was close to tears. "I told you I won't go anywhere with him again."

"But then, if my assumption is correct, he'll just find some other girl. Maybe your friend Jennie."

"Jennie doesn't look childish. And she's too smart—" She stopped.

"You're not?"

They had arrived at the supermarket. She swung around to him. "I don't think you should be questioning me like this without my mother here."

"Maybe not." He reached into his wallet. "I'm going to give you a card. If you change your mind and decide to tell me your friend's name, I want you to call me. If he's innocent, no harm will be done. If he's not—you want Lisa's killer caught, don't you?"

"Of course." She was crying now. She yanked the card from his hand, wiped at her eyes with the side of her hand and darted into the supermarket.

He stood there thinking, I may have scared her off. Now she may not tell me anything. On the other hand, I've given her something to think about. Dissatisfied, he walked back to his car. Putting a tail on a twelve-year-old seemed oddly decadent.

35

Ruth arrived at Libby's at around three on Saturday. Unable to reach Joel by phone all weekend, finally she had driven to his house. No one answered her ring. She was uneasy; it was as if he had decided *Bible Story* was finished and had already left town in search of other work.

"That's nonsense," Libby said. She was growing a little weary of men and their unpredictability.

"I know. I keep telling myself that. Where's Kurt?"

"He left to take the kids to the playgound. He was out all morning, just got back." She grinned. "He's making amends. "I thought I'd grab the chance to run over to my mother's. Come on, you like Alicia."

They took Libby's car. "Where in hell can he have gone?" Ruth said.

"Join the club. Who knows where any of them is ever?" She was silent as they swung off the freeway into the access road that led to the mobile home park. Funny, she thought, how much time we devote to these things, worrying about whether we're loved, untangling misunderstandings, just trying to communicate simple things to each other. Kurt and I. Libby and Joel. Poor Mother, she had to give up on it altogether. After a while she said, "Alicia's depressed, too."

"Your mother? Why?"

"Years ago some friend of hers had a child who was pretty brutally raped, and that whole business of the little girl has set her thinking about it again. She went through it all with the woman, stayed with her. I remember she left me with a neighbor. I was fourteen and really didn't need to be with anyone, but she was petrified that I'd be the next. She left all sorts of instructions about me; I didn't know what was going on, but I remember how creepy the whole thing was. She was awfully depressed for weeks after."

"Did they catch the man?"

"No. They thought it was an adolescent boy, I can't recall why, but they never tracked him down."

"It must be awful never to be able to vent your anger. Even if all he was given was a light sentence, knowing he'd been caught would help."

"Maybe. I don't think anything really helps. Can you imagine what it would be like if it were Kate or Cory? Or Barbara?"

"I knew I shouldn't have dropped in on you." They pulled up in front of Alicia's mobile home.

"I'm sorry. But I thought you should be told, in case Alicia starts in on it again. One thing, this has gotten her out of the house. She's decided she won't hang around thinking about it, so she's going places in the evenings. She used to be a terrible stick-in-the-mud, sat around waiting for me to suggest an occasional movie or something." She turned to look at the house next door.

"That's where your boyfriend lives."

"My *boyfriend*?" As she spoke, Robert Carter pulled his car into the carport.

"Good-looking," decided Ruth, peering at him as they got out of the car.

"Hi." Libby walked toward him. "Come meet my friend Ruth."

158

"Oh, yes, you mentioned her." He joined them beside Libby's car. "You're the friend of the filmmaker?"

"My claim to fame."

"I didn't mean that. It's just that I met him at work. He came in to see Nora. Bright guy. Interesting sounding film, too."

"He's bright enough," conceded Ruth, grudging.

Robert cast a puzzled glance her way. "Visiting Mother?" he asked Libby.

"Yes. She's in the doldrums."

"Oh?"

"That little girl who was killed in the park."

"Oh." After a minute he added, "She knew her?"

"No. Don't you remember? She told us about it the day—"

"Oh, her friend's daughter. Yes."

"Actually, though"—Libby turned to Ruth—"Mother did know Lisa Margolin. She subbed for her class for a week one time."

Robert Carter hesitated. "Anything I can do?"

"No, but thanks for offering, Robert."

He stood for a moment longer, looking at her, and then said, "Well, good to meet you, Ruth," and turned toward his own house.

"He's luscious," Ruth said. "Kurt better watch out. And the way he looks at you."

Libby flushed. "He doesn't look at me any way."

"Oh, doesn't he? Hungry, I'd say. You know, Lib, you could really get into trouble with someone like that. You'd better think whether you want Kurt or not."

Alicia met them at the sliding glass doors.

"Hi, Mother. I brought one of your favorite people. You look good," she added, looking closely at her mother.

"I feel all right. Come in, see what I'm doing." She had begun an intricate piece of quilting.

Alicia seemed in wholly good spirits; Ruth could see how deeply Libby was affected by that. On their way home she commented. "You feel better now, don't you?"

"I do."

"And that quilting. She designed that?"

"Yes. She's really good. She could earn a living doing quilt designs if she wanted to. But she loves kids—teaching is a natural for her."

"Lib?"

"Yes."

"Are you really interested in this Robert Carter?"

"I—I wouldn't have been. I mean, I didn't feel a need for anyone else till all this business with Kurt started. Now I find I'm—well, attracted, but scared. I don't want to get into anything I can't handle. I think Robert likes me."

"That's obvious enough. But it would be a problem for him, too, if you got involved."

"You mean because he works for Kurt."

"Yes. And then there's the business of your marriage. And the kids."

"I know. If only Kurt would *talk* to me about things, we could work them out, but he clams up and refuses to discuss anything. He goes into a rage if I question him."

"I can't imagine Kurt in a rage."

"Believe me, he's quite capable of it."

"You can't go along like this, distrusting each other, neither of you knowing where the other is when you're out. It's no way to live."

"My mother told me you'd have advice for me."

"And you told her I couldn't even manage my own affairs."

Libby laughed. "Right on the button. That's just what I told her."

"But with Joel and me it's different. Ours is just a little—spat, nothing that will really affect our relationship."

"You're sure? You've been acting as though you weren't."

"Lib, don't. I'm not sure; that's the trouble. But I am sure you should do something to get straight with Kurt. Unless you've really had it with him. Have you?"

"I don't know. That's the truth, I just don't know. I don't like the person he's become in the last couple of months. I don't even know that person."

"Would he go to a marriage counselor?"

"Kurt? Never. Can you imagine it?"

160

"Have you broached the subject?"

"What's the use? He'd just be madder."

"You don't know."

"I do. I know Kurt."

"Now *that*," said Ruth, "I seriously doubt. You don't have any idea where he is half the time; you don't understand his friendship with this Nora Crane; you can't talk to him. How is it that you know him so well?"

They had reached Libby's house. Libby leaned her hands on the steering wheel and laid her head against them. When she raised it, her eyes were wet. "Damn him! *Damn* him!" she said. "I'm going to get him to talk. I'm going to issue an ultimatum."

"Libby—"

"You're right, it's no way to live—all this tension. And it can't be good for the kids. I'm talking to my mother and my friends—at least to you and Robert—and I'm not talking to the one person who could help untangle this mess we've got ourselves into." She got out of the car.

Ruth stood hesitantly beside her. "Look, I didn't mean to—"

"You didn't do anything, Ruth. We've been building toward this for weeks. You helped, really you did."

Ruth hugged her. "Maybe. Now I'll get into my own car and go try to find Joel. See what I can do with my own problems, since I'm so good at solving yours."

Libby laughed. "Joel'll be there, full of remorse and furious because you were out and he couldn't tell you."

"We'll see," said Ruth.

36

Ever since her encounter with Pedersen, Meredith had been uneasy. She tried the journal as a way of understanding what she felt, but it didn't clarify her emotions. It was a relief, though, she decided, to tell someone—some *thing* that she was uncomfortable. Sunday morning she took out the book and began to write.

Sunday, April 17

Yesterday when I went to the store for my mother, there outside was that detective, Mr. Pedersen, waiting for me. He'd just seen me with HIM on Cliff Drive, and he wanted to warn me against going places with somebody who might be Lisa's murderer. That's crazy—he isn't a murderer. But it made me feel creepy just the same. I don't know why. I wouldn't tell Mr. Pedersen the name of the person I was with—that would be like saying, go act like he's a murderer! I don't know. Maybe I shouldn't meet him on Tuesday. I told the detective I wouldn't and I usually don't lie, but I guess HE matters more to me than some old detective. The other thing is that I don't much want to go to Richards West. That's where Lisa was killed and I haven't been over there since. He'll wait and be mad and maybe worried, but when he calls me I can explain.

But what can I explain? I can't very well tell him the detective told me not to go anyplace with him. Maybe I should tell him what Mr. Pedersen said, and then I'd find out for sure. That sounds as though I'm not sure, and I am. And I did ask him about Lisa that first time. He didn't even remember her. The whole thing is so silly.

But I think that detective put dumb ideas in my head. I don't know. I'm all mixed up. I don't know what to do.

And I'm going to have my period again soon. My mother says about every twenty-eight days. She told me sometimes before she has hers, she gets all blue and feels like crying—it has something to do with something she calls edema. (I'm not sure if I spelled that right.) Maybe that's why I feel so mixed up and sort of depressed. That could be it.

Oh, yes, something else. That boy I rode back on the bus with—I won't say his name, either, just in case (I can just hear Sean making fun of me)—anyway, he called me the other day after school. We talked for about two hours! Good thing my mother wasn't here. She'd have freaked out. I like him—he's not special like HIM, but he's fun to talk to. It's too bad men make boys seem so callow.

37

Before she had finished the test, Meredith realized she had done terribly. English, she thought as she left the room, English, my best subject. She wondered what the failure would do to her grade. For Meredith, failure was unfamiliar. I'll just have to *deal* with it, she thought as she walked to her locker, English being the last class of the day. But her mother's response to problems seemed hollow; in fact, she didn't feel she could deal with it. Walking through the halls on her way out of the building, she recited to herself the answers she should have given and hadn't.

She knew. It's that detective, she grumbled to herself as she hurried down the steps to avoid being caught up with by a classmate. He got me all upset and now I can't even think straight in school. Or out of it. She still felt mixed-up, confused as to whether she should meet her friend in the park. Not meeting him was admitting to some uncertainty, and she felt no uncertainty, did she? She recalled the way he had twinkled at her and their laughter over the silly pelicans. Why was she so muddled up about the whole thing?

At home, she found no one in. There was a relief in that, no need to explain to her mother about the test or to prepare her for a possible change in her grade. She went into her room and closed the door. After a few minutes she sighed and dug out her journal.

Monday, April 18

I almost told my mother. It was last night, Sunday, and I was sitting in the living room with her. She was in a chair reading a book called Jumping the Queue—*and I asked her what a queue was and she said a line, like in a supermarket. Anyway, she kept giggling—chuckling, I guess, is a better word for it, but I noticed she kept checking her watch. I figured she was waiting for Kurt and that maybe it would be a good time to tell her.*

I wasn't sure how to tell her. After a while I said, "Mother, do you think grown-ups"—then I changed it to adults— "are ever interested in children who aren't their own kids?" She kind of half looked up from her book and said, "Of course." She didn't sound as though she'd really heard me, so I said, "Why should they be?" and she said, "Be what?" I said, "Interested in children." She seemed to be paying more attention then and she said, "Children are quick minded, lively. Adults like that. Are you feeling neglected by someone?" She said it in a sort of sarcastic voice.

I was so mad at the idea that she thought I was feeling neglected by somebody that I said, "No, never mind. I'm not feeling neglected." She seemed sorry she'd said that and then she asked, "Is anything wrong, Meredith? Why did you ask me that?" That was when I almost told her. Instead I said, "I wondered if some grown-up made Lisa think he liked her." My mother got up and came over and hugged me. "You're still so upset over that, aren't you, darling?" she said, and then Sean came in.

Sean's been really creepy lately. He keeps watching me, as though he's deciding something—to say something or do something. But he never says it or does it. He kind of flopped down in a chair when he came in this time and looked at me and said, "And what is little sister up to?" in this knowing way. He can't know anything about my meeting HIM (gosh, it's getting harder and harder to remember not to say his name), but it was as though he sort of hit the nail on the head. Anyway, my mother began on him about where he'd been and what he'd been doing and forgot all about me, and I went into my bedroom.

That was yesterday. Tomorrow I have to decide whether to meet HIM. Today I was—my head was so full of thinking about it that I failed that English test. I know I did—I usually know just how I do on tests, almost to the percent right, and I know I failed this one. I could kill that dumb detective for telling me those things. I can't believe HE could have hurt Lisa. It's impossible. But that Mr. Pedersen somehow put doubts in my head, maybe not about HIM but about the park, which I don't much want to visit and about—oh, I don't know—things. I guess I shouldn't go tomorrow. But how can I explain? I don't want him to be mad at me.

As I wrote that, I realized what that means. I'll have to go. If he gets mad at me and if he thinks I can't be counted on to show up when we have a "date," maybe I won't see him anymore. That would mean losing one of the most important people in my life. Gosh, what a mess. This must be what authors mean when they talk about being in a quandry. I'll go tomorrow.

It didn't seem to have helped much, writing, today. She wrapped the book in the clean panties she reserved for that purpose and put it back in the hamper.

She wished her father were there. She could tell him and he'd know what to do.

38

The Kurt-Nora business had hardened into a rigid silence. Libby had done nothing about the promised ultimatum. They were polite before the children.

"Let me know," Libby said coldly the morning after a night spent sleeping in the guest room, "whether you'll be in for dinner. If you're going to be out, I'm getting a sitter."

"To go where?" His voice was rough.

"I'll find someplace, don't worry." She could see the two children anxiously watching her face.

He glanced at them. "I'll be in." She regarded it as a modest triumph yet, strangely, she was disappointed. Had she been looking forward to—she didn't let Robert linger in her mind.

The door closed behind him and she looked at the kitchen clock. "Time to go," she said. "Get your lunch boxes. She went to the closet for their jackets. The days were being ruined by this pitched battle between them. I could be sweetly reasonable, use I-messages—but immediately something rose up in her in protest. Let him come to me, she thought, let him come to me. Women do all the placating. Not this time. Either he comes to me or I do something about that ultimatum.

She was irritable as she helped the children into their jackets. They knew something was going on.

After dropping them, driving back to her empty house, she considered. The house would be lonely. She could drop in on her mother, not discuss what had evolved but just see her. That is, if her mother wasn't out subbing; usually on Mondays she didn't work. She turned the car in the direction of the mobile-home park.

Her mother, still in her bathrobe, was visible through the sliding door, sitting over a cup of coffee and the morning paper. She sighed as she greeted Libby. "Hi, sweetie. I don't know why I begin my day with the news. It's enough to depress anybody. This world is in a hell of a mess."

And my life is in another, Libby wanted to cry; help me. Instead she said, "Any coffee in the pot?"

"Yes. Let me heat it." She took the coffee pot into her tiny kitchen. "Everything all right? How'd you happen to come by so early?"

"You sound as though you don't want me." Libby looked around her mother's house—did you think of a mobile home as a house? All the funiture was familiar to her; she had grown up with most of it. The old chair, once a lovely burnt orange, now a faded tannish color, the mahogany gateleg table with its four chairs, the formerly comfortable sofa that had relaxed into squishiness. "What happened to the etchings?" she called.

Her mother reappeared, pot in hand. "What etchings? I haven't changed anything."

"The ones you had of European scenes; they used to be over the old sideboard."

"Oh, those. God, I haven't thought of them in years. They weren't very good; your father was just sentimental about them. They reminded him of his youthful grand tour or something."

"Where are they?"

"I got rid of them when I moved in here, gave them to Goodwill."

168

"You should have given them to me. Or at least asked if I wanted them." A terrible sense of loss engulfed her.

"It never crossed my mind. God, those old things, I'd never think you'd use them." She paused. "Did you want them because they remind you of Daddy?"

"No. I guess I wouldn't have taken them if you'd offered them." Forcing the emotion away, she accepted the cup.

"Have the English muffin; I don't want another. What's happening with Kurt?" She studied her daughter's face narrowly.

"You mean what I told you?"

"Yes. Did you find out anything?"

"He was visiting that woman to help with her teenage son. The boy's into drugs, she thinks."

"That sounds legitimate."

"Maybe. I have my doubts."

"So things are tense between you."

Libby laughed. "Well, they aren't comfortable between us. I'm damned if I'll—oh, I don't want to talk about it."

"I see."

"What do you see?"

"That you don't want to talk about it."

"But"—Libby turned to her mother piteously—"I do want to talk about it. I don't know what's going on. You know, the other night when Kurt was out—I suppose he stayed out just to show me he wouldn't be dominated—"

"You're hardly the dominating sort."

"Apparently he thinks so. Anyway, when he was out, I came over here. By the way, where have you been lately?"

Her mother laughed. "I told you I decided not to sit around here."

"Well, that's exactly the way I felt, too. When Kurt went out, I decided I wasn't going to hang around waiting for him. So I came over here."

"And I was inconveniently out."

"No, this time you were in. I didn't come to see you; I came to see your neighbor."

"Lorna? What on earth for?"

"Not Lorna, your other neighbor. Robert."

"But you barely know him."

"I know him now. I stopped in there one evening when I was looking for you and then another time. And I visited him the night I'm talking about. While Kurt was out."

Her mother pressed her lips together. "You're playing with fire."

"Oh, Mother, that corny old cliché. I'm not—we aren't having an affair or anything. I just wanted to be around a man who doesn't prefer some other woman to me."

Her mother said nothing.

"I don't mean—I don't know who he prefers, really. I don't know anything about his personal life. But he obviously considers me attractive and we had a good time together, talking. And you needn't look that way. He didn't touch me."

"If he had?"

"Well, he didn't." Except for a warm handclasp, she thought, and then, God, I must be hard up, thinking of that as an erotic gesture.

"Well, since you've told me, I don't think it's a good idea. For one thing, he works for your husband."

"Mother, I know that." Libby set down her cup. "I didn't tell you because I want your approval. Or even"—she added more gently—"your opinion. I just needed to tell you."

"And where do you think this is all going, Kurt with another woman, you with another man? Do you really think that's going to resolve anything? You do have two children to consider."

"I know. If we didn't have the kids—"

"What? You'd divorce Kurt? You haven't had enough of divorce?"

"That was your divorce, not mine. And I know what it does to kids; I know what it did to me. But I'm so furious with him, so angry, I can hardly look at him. And he doesn't talk about it."

"Have you tried?"

"That one evening, after I went to see her."

"You went to see the woman?"

"Yes. I didn't mean to tell you. She seems perfectly pleasant; in fact, I rather liked her, and she doesn't seem to be trying to wrest him away from me or anything dramatic like that. As a matter of fact, she seems stuck in her own problems. I suppose Kurt did go there to help. She says he's never made a pass."

"And you told him you'd gone?"

"Yes. Naturally he was livid. He wouldn't discuss it at all. I haven't tried since. Last night—last night I slept in the guest room."

"Well, I can see where this is going."

"Not necessarily. I will talk with him, eventually, I suppose. Or he'll talk with me."

"Have you discussed this with Ruth?"

"Yes." Libby suddenly felt very tired. "She has her own problems."

"You should talk to her, I told you. She'll talk some sense into you, even if I can't."

Libby laughed wearily. "Oh yes. She's full of sage advice for me." She picked up her bag and bent to kiss her mother. "Don't worry, it'll all straighten itself out. We both love the kids too much to do anything bad to them."

That's true, she thought as she walked down the path, glancing at Robert's silent house. It's the kids that matter. We have to get things back on track. She looked again at the Carter house. It looks so welcoming, she thought. Unlike home.

39

Meredith closed her door, locked it and listened. Her mother and brother were "having a talk," as her mother put it. To Meredith it sounded more like a fight. Her brother had been acting crazy again; perhaps her mother had gotten wind of it. Just the night before when she was already in bed, lights out, he had come into her room and stood and looked at her. She had pretended to be asleep but she found his long scrutiny caused her to feel crawly all over. She lay, tense and silent, eyes open just a slit, ready to leap from the bed and scream if he came closer. He took one step toward her and then, just as she was about to cry out, turned and went away.

Taking out her journal, she sighed. She felt as though she were wading in some substance that kept sucking at her; it wasn't a good feeling and she couldn't understand it. She picked up her pen.

Tuesday, April 19

*I'm doing something different today. I'm writing before
school. It's Tuesday, the day, and something funny has
happened. Not funny, strange. HE called. It was last night
and I got to the phone first. I don't know what he'd have
said if my mother had picked it up, probably that he was
calling her. Anyway, he said something had come up and
he couldn't meet me till later, and we'd have to cut our
walk short because of that. I started to say I couldn't make
it at all and then he laughed and said something about not
blaming me if I called it off and I felt so guilty I didn't.
Now I don't know what to do, whether to go or not. I don't
believe he had anything to do with Lisa, I don't know why
I feel so uneasy.*

*I could talk to him, tell him I'm—not worried, exactly, but
uncomfortable. He's easy to talk to. But what if he was the
person Lisa went with? I remember she had a crush on
him after we went up to the magazine for our visit. Could
he have been the one? They say criminals are very smart
about fooling you. He couldn't. Every time I think of him
smiling at me like that, I know he couldn't. I'll go this
afternoon.*

*Now I'd better get to school. I just heard Sean slam the
door; he's left. And I'd better unlock my door; my mother
hates it when I lock myself in here.*

She buried the journal in the hamper and picked up her
schoolbooks.

40

Meredith met him at four-thirty; the park was still lively with ball players, walkers, women coming from the pool.

He looked distracted "Sorry about the switch in time. We'll have about an hour. When do you have to be back for dinner?"

"I should be in by five."

"Well, then, a half hour. What do you sat we go down by the stream?"

"No. Let's watch the ball game."

"How can we talk and watch the ball game?"

She looked at him and away quickly. "We don't have much time, anyway. For talking, I mean." Then she added, "Did you have something special you wanted to talk about?"

"No." He looked over her head. "Let's watch the game."

They sat on a bench next to the field. She carefully kept her distance.

"Is something the matter, Meredith?"

"No." She cleared her throat. "What should be the matter?"

"I don't know. He moved closer to her and she edged slightly away. "Something *is* the matter."

"No. I guess it's just—Lisa was killed in this park. It reminds me of her."

"Hell, I'm sorry. I never thought."

How could you not? she thought.

"We needn't stay here," he went on. "We could drive up to campus and walk there. Or go down to the water."

"This is fine. I just told you why I acted—different."

"I'm sorry, Meredith. You must think me terribly unfeeling." He placed his hand over hers.

She squirmed and rearranged her sweater, sliding her hand out from under his. He did sound sorry, really sorry. She put her own hand out and touched his, a fleeting birdtouch. "I don't think that."

"You do." He sounded depressed. "I forget you were close to—Lisa."

"She was one of my two best friends. I"—a tear rolled down her cheek and she rubbed at it angrily—"miss her. I keep thinking I'll call her up and tell her something, and then I remember she's not there." She turned her face up to his. He was studying her sadly. "You know?"

"I can imagine." The ball game went on, forgotten by them. "Can you imagine what made somebody *do* that to her?"

"Yes, but I don't think you'd understand. People do terrible things in their necessity."

"What do you mean in their necessity?"

He was looking off over the park. "That's a pretty grown-up concept for you. People do things they don't want to sometimes. Things they don't mean to."

"You sound as though you're making excuses for him."

"No." He shook his head, his face still sad. "I'm making no excuses for him." He stood up. "I think maybe we should cut this visit short. Where did you leave your bike?"

"I don't—we don't have to—"

"I think it's better."

They turned and walked toward the slender tree to which she had chained her bike. "Are you mad at me?" she said.

"No. Next time we'll choose a different place."

"You're sure you're not mad?" The thought of the loss of him as a friend filled her with panic.

"Sure." He turned and smiled at her, the warm smile that reminded her of her father. "Let's make it this weekend. We'll go off somewhere by ourselves and have a picnic. I'll bring the picnic. Is it a date?"

Relief swept her. "Oh, yes. Saturday?"

He grinned. "Right after the wash cycle. Let's meet at the campus library—you know your way there? In that downstairs patio. Eleven-thirty? There are good paths and we'll find a place and sit and eat. What do you like to eat?"

"Oh, anything. And pickles," she added.

He laughed, a wonderful sound to her ears. "Anything and pickles it will be. Off you go. See you Saturday."

As she rode toward home, she thought, I acted terrible. That policeman almost made me lose my friend. I'm so glad he isn't mad.

Impatient as she was to get to her journal, Meredith had first to dry the dinner dishes. Her mother didn't have a dishwasher like all her friends' mothers; she said it was unnecessary with only three people in the house. She always added, with a meaningful glance at Sean, "When there *are* three people."

Sean had not met Meredith's eye when she had seen him that morning, and then he had left for school while she was still in her room. She wondered if he knew she had been awake the night before when he came in; maybe her breathing was wrong and had given her away. It was creepy, but Sean seemed to have some special sense; he seemed to know things no one ever told him. It wasn't that he was reading her journal. She was sure of that—she had developed a particular way of wrapping the journal and always found it wrapped just in that way. Besides he wasn't really around that much.

One thing she had learned about Sean was that he didn't do crack, smoke crack. Did you smoke it or use a needle? Anyway, she had figured out that it was only pot he used. Maybe pills. But not crack. She had found out through a telephone conversation she had overheard. She had almost not known it was Sean talking on the phone, he sounded so different. He was saying to his friend, "No, man, stay away from that crack shit. It's really dangerous. I'm telling you, you'll get a habit. It's not like grass."

Meredith didn't quite know how to take her new knowledge of him. In a way it was upsetting. It made the things Sean did to her and his attitude toward her *real* in a way they wouldn't be if he were on drugs. Heavy drugs. But maybe pot and speed and stuff like that also made you behave that way. All the kids at school said pot wasn't anything; no worse than drinking beer. Some of the kids at her junior high school did both. Sean did both.

She put the last cup away and went into her bedroom. Tonight she was excited in a different way, as though she had gone through something and come out all right. She supposed it was because she had gone to meet HIM today full of all those strange feelings the detective had made her have, and when she left him, she knew her trust in him was not only restored but stronger then ever. If it weren't silly, she'd think she was in love with him. A twelve-year-old in love with a grown man was pretty ridiculous, but she thought about him all the time and couldn't wait to see him—wasn't that what love felt like? Yet sometimes he reminded her of her father. You couldn't be in love with your father.

In fact, tonight she felt she hated her father.

She had seen him that day. It had been as she biked home from the park; she had passed him on the street walking with his new wife. She had begun to brake—her father hadn't yet noticed her—when his wife turned and Meredith saw. Daddy's wife was pregnant. She had sped past them, almost crashing into a parked car, and ridden home as though someone were chasing her.

First he had married someone else, crushing her hope that

one day he and her mother might live together again, and now they were going to have a baby. If he had a new baby, her father would really forget all about her. Whatever it was she and Sean had done that had made him not want to stay and be their father didn't matter anymore. He was planning to start over and have better children this time. The thought depressed her too much to think about.

She took out her journal.

Tuesday, April 19 (again!)

I went today. I was very nervous—I've never felt that way with him before. It was all those things that Mr. Pedersen said to me—I kept thinking, What if he was the person Lisa went with. Now that seems crazy. I don't know how I could even have thought it. We sat and watched the ball game and when he asked why I was acting funny and I told him because Lisa was killed there, he seemed really sorry. He said it hadn't crossed his mind. For me the park will always be the place where Lisa was killed. I don't think I'll ever feel the same about it.

I asked him how he thought someone could do that to her and he looked very—grave is the word, I think. He said it was somebody's necessity—I didn't understand exactly what he meant. How could anybody need to kill Lisa? Anyway, we talked for a while and then he said we should go. For a minute I was scared that he wouldn't want to meet me anymore. I don't know what I'd have done if that happened—I can't imagine what life would be like if I didn't have our time together to look forward to. But he said he wasn't mad and smiled at me in that way that reminds me of Daddy, and he said we should meet "right after the wash cycle" (he was making a joke) at 11:30 on Saturday, up at the university library. He said there are some wonderful walks up there. I really can't wait! I feel so different about him, as though I'd—I don't know, tested him, I guess, and he passed the test. That's not really it, but it's sort of like that.

Tonight I've been thinking about Daddy. I get such a sad

feeling when I think about him. It's like something is pulling me down. (I don't make sense tonight—Anne would disown me.) His wife is going to have a baby. I keep wondering why he didn't come over and tell Sean and me—we could go visit it. I like babies. They have feathery little heads like birds, and they smell delicious, all powdery. I held a little baby that a friend of my mother's from work had, and I just wanted to keep on cuddling it. Imagine, I could have one, now that I've finally had my period.

For a moment she sat dreamily looking off into space. The idea surprised her, that she could have a baby, too, just like her father's wife. She'd never thought of it before. It would be nice to have a warm pink little thing like her mother's friend had, but—she sighed—it would be an awful responsibility. She couldn't imagine what she'd do if it cried. Her mother's friend's baby had cried and although its mother had held it and jiggled it and offered it a bottle, it went right on crying. Meredith had wanted to cover her ears. A baby crying was a scary, awful sound. She guessed it was just as well that she didn't have one.

She folded the panties around the journal and deposited it at the bottom of the hamper. She still had her homework to do; she reached for her history notebook and put small children and pregnant wives out of her mind.

41

The phone rang while they were having dinner. Pedersen laid his napkin on the table.

It was the woman, one of them, who had identified Lisa as she hurried down the path. He came to immediate attention. She was talking fast.

"We had just picked up our canvas carryalls and headed for the door and Gerry's car, when I saw them. I said, 'Look there, Gerry.'"

"Saw them? Who did you see?"

"A little girl getting on her bike. I said, 'Isn't that person with her the one we saw with—' and Gerry squinted. She wears glasses but she didn't have them on. The she said, 'Edith, you're getting paranoid.' But I don't think I am. He looked the same to me, sort of the same shape. And dark hair. Maybe he didn't walk exactly the same; I couldn't tell that."

"Go on."

"Gerry made fun of me. She said if that was the man, he'd

180

avoid the place like the plague. I suppose that's true. Unless he was returning to the scene of the crime."

"What did you do?"

"Well, Gerry said I think about the whole thing too much. She said I liked being an eyewitness. We weren't eyewitnesses, were we? We didn't see anybody do anything. Anyway, after we left I thought about it and I decided I should use that card you gave me—I had it on my kitchen bulletin board—and call you. I didn't tell Gerry."

"I think I'd better come by to talk with you. I'll be there in about fifteen minutes."

Freda asked him nothing. After a moment he grinned and said, "Freda, your restraint is remarkable."

"My restraint." She looked at him, surprised. "You've never complimented me on that before."

"You're bursting to ask about that phone call and about where I'm going tonight and you haven't said a word."

She turned an innocent face to him. "You said not to ask."

"I know I did. Pretty hard on you, though, isn't it, not asking?"

"I won't develop an ulcer, if that's what you're thinking."

He laughed. "No, with you it would take more than that." He finished his dessert. "When I get back I'll tell you all about it."

She raised her eyebrows. "Restraint seems to get results around here."

He laughed again. "It's the tension that gets results. I can't endure another minute of it."

E dith Hollister lived in a tract house on a street lined with similar tract houses. Although the exterior did not distinguish the house, inside she had made an effort at uniqueness. The living room had been subjected to a color scheme, with each object matched to some other object. The colors, purple, rose and an unusual shade of yellow-green, were cheerful enough in themselves, although Pedersen could not imagine living with them, but the meticulousness with which the ashtrays picked up the yellow-green, with which the cushions echoed the precise shade of rose, discomfited him. He found himself looking around for something wildly discordant—a brilliant blue footstool, a bright red book on a table. There was none.

There was a scent of cooked lamb in the house. He sat down. "You've finished dinner? I'm not interrupting?"

She shook her head and squirmed a little in the soft chair. "My friend Gerry says I didn't see anything, and maybe I didn't. I told you that?"

"You did. But something caught your eye. What was it? Tell it to me as you saw it, not as your friend did."

A gleam of satisfaction crept into her eyes. "She tends to be rather bossy. Well, what I thought I saw was that same man, the one who was with the little girl. He had his back to me, same as before, and he had the dark hair and—well, the shape of him seemed the same."

"What was he doing?"

"He was saying good-bye to a young girl." She looked down at her hands. "About the same age as Lisa Margolin. That was what made me notice."

"And the girl was—?"

"Was? Oh, you mean what was she doing? She was unlocking a bike she had chained to a tree. Then she got on the bike and sailed off and he waved good-bye and walked away."

He was aware of a hollowness in his belly. "Did you get a glimpse of his face?"

"No, they were a little distance away. If Gerry hadn't been so sure it wasn't the man, we could have followed and got a good look at him."

"You didn't see him get into a car?"

"No. I just saw him walk off. I should have followed him, shouldn't I?"

"It would have been good if you could have done it in your car, without attracting attention. Maybe you'll have another chance." He paused. "I suppose you didn't get a good look at the girl, either?"

"There was something—what was it?"

He asked, knowing it would be wiser to let her struggle

through to an answer, but unable to resist, "The color of her hair?"

"That's it. She had red hair."

"I see." He sat silent for a moment. "Thank you for telling me."

"You—something I said bothers you, doesn't it?"

He smiled. "You're perceptive. All of it bothers me, all of it. But you may have helped more than you think."

She accompanied him to the door. Now that he was leaving the room, he could be generous. "Nice place," he said, smiling down at her. "Nice colors."

42

At her desk, Meredith pulled her journal toward her, her body tense with purpose. She picked up her pen.

Wednesday, April 20

Something happened. That policeman came to see me. He had a policewoman with him (I've never seen one before except on TV—just meter maids), but my mother was out and so was Sean and I wasn't sure I should let him in. So I just stood in the doorway and talked with him. It certainly seems as if he's following me or something.

The thing he said—asked—was if I had gone over to Richards West yesterday. I can't imagine how he knew. I was only there about a half hour—he must have been following me. When I asked him, he said, no, but that I'd been seen. He didn't say who saw me. He said my red hair makes me noticeable. Identifiable, I think he said. I didn't know what to say. I wanted to tell him I hadn't been there at all, but he's a policeman and I was scared to lie. So I

*said I had biked through. Then he asked me who I was
with. I wasn't about to tell him that, so I said, looking as
innocent as I could, "Nobody. I was by myself." He asked
if there was a man with me. I looked very surprised and
said, "A man! What would a man be doing with me?" He
looked as though he didn't believe me and he said, "You
were with a man friend the other day." Then he went on.
"Meredith, I can't seem to impress on you that you may be
putting yourself in danger." I kind of shivered, he said it
so seriously.*

*I just don't believe it—he's got HIM mixed up with
somebody else. Anyway, I said, "I know that. I was all
alone yesterday. I'm telling the truth." After a while he
said, "You don't seem like a girl who would lie (I squirmed
a little, even though I had my hand in my jeans pocket and
my fingers crossed), so I'll believe you. But, Meredith, I
want you to remember, don't"—and then he repeated
it—"don't allow yourself to be in any secluded place,
anyplace where there aren't lots of people, if you're with
your friend." He didn't say who he meant by my friend,
but I guess in the end, despite saying that about the kind
of girl I am, he knew I was lying.*

*This whole thing is crazy and it gives me the creeps. I'm
supposed to believe HE would hurt me and that maybe he
hurt Lisa. I just don't believe it and I think that policeman
is awful for trying to make me not trust him. I'm not
dumb. I know whether somebody's being straight with me.
I'm going Saturday and that's that, and if that policeman
wants to follow along behind us, he can. I don't think he'll
do that, though, with all that stuff in the papers about how
the police force is "seriously diminished" and every extra
man is being assigned to the mall. Anyway, if we were
followed, we'd slip away.*

She reread what she had written. Then she added a note.

*Sean's been hanging around lately, too. I don't know why
I'm so interesting to everybody all of a sudden. He seems to
be trying to make up to me, all palsy-walsy after all the*

strange things he's been doing. I'm scared to let him hang around my room when Mother isn't here. I lock my door even though she doesn't like us to do that. I think that policeman ought to follow Sean! That makes more sense than bugging me all the time. He's the weirdo creep. When I wrote that, suddenly I felt very sad. I used to think Sean was everything. He was my big brother who helped me when I got stuck on arithmetic problems or my bike wouldn't work right. Now I feel as though he's some stranger—that sounds melodramatic, but it's true. I'm actually afraid of him, not that he'll hit me or anything, but afraid of something—I don't know how to say it— something in him. I was glad to learn he wasn't on crack, but that doesn't seem to make him any less weird. Oh dear, my life is just a mess.

Tom called me again. (Oh, I wasn't going to say his name—the boy on the bus. But I guess it doesn't matter.) We talked for a long time.

I have my period again. This time I only ache. Maybe that's from LIFE.

43

"Lunch," Kurt said. "You never meet me for lunch."

"Well, I'm coming down today. I have something to tell you. What time?"

She could hear him rustling papers on his desk. "I'm *busy* today. Can't it wait till evening?"

"No. What time?"

There was a long silence. "What time do you pick up the kids?"

"I made other arrangements for them. What time?"

"God. I suppose one will be all right."

"I'll pick you up at one." Libby hung up. Her determination to face him out had fueled her anger. She picked up the phone again.

"Ruth? I've set up a date for the confrontation. Finally," she said. "Have you heard from Joel?"

"About an hour ago. I was in conference and he called. I had to leave the meeting."

"What did he say? Where's he been?"

"He didn't talk. He's coming over tonight. I must have looked like a fool when I went back to my meeting, I was grinning so."

"So he was all right. I told you they take care of themselves." She paused. "I'll let you know how things go." She hung up.

Kurt was waiting for her, his desk if not clear at least orderly, as though he had put aside all other concerns. Robert was nowhere in evidence. Kurt took her arm as they left the office. "Where to?" he said.

"Rachel's. I made a reservation. They have a garden with tables far apart."

He relinquished her arm. "This sounds solemn."

"Not solemn. We need privacy."

He followed her to her car. She drove.

Eggplant parmesan was featured. They ordered it. "And wine," Kurt said. "Bring us a half liter of your driest white." As soon as the waitress moved away, he said, "All right. Let's have it."

"It? *It* is this: I want to know everything about you and Nora Crane—and about us. What's wrong with me that you need her? And this time, Kurt, I mean it. If we don't get this straightened out, I'm going to leave you."

He started slightly, as though his chair had been jarred. Then his face twisted into a smile. "You're going home to Mother?"

"I'm serious, Kurt. Deadly."

He waited while the waitress poured wine from the tall cylinder into their glasses, set it on the table and hurried off. Then he ran a hand over his face. "I don't know. I don't know what's wrong, but something is, Libby. I don't seem to have any—sexual desire anymore."

"For me?"

He met her eyes. "For you."

"And Nora Crane?" She was surprised her voice was so steady.

"Not for her, either."

"Then why go there?"

He sighed deeply. "It's—it was a way not to go home, not to face up to you. And I do like her kids."

"I thought you didn't like her son."

"Well, I'm trying to help her with him. I was. And I—like her daughter."

"That seems like a pretty odd reason for spending evening after evening with her. Doesn't she expect something of you, too—Nora?"

"I suppose she does. She's never broached the subject, as though it really doesn't matter, but I've caught her looking at me oddly—she probably thinks I'm nuts. The way you do."

"Why don't you go to a doctor?"

"What about? Oh, you mean the sex. What could he do?"

"Maybe you need hormones. Maybe your health is failing. That's what doctors are for—to tell you what's causing things."

"I'll stop going to Nora Crane's. I have stopped, in fact."

"Every time you're late or out on a weekend, I think you're there."

"Will it help to know I'm not?"

"Not unless something happens to alter the situation with us."

"You mean the sex?"

"Of course I mean the sex. What do you think?" She looked around and lowered her voice. "I'm a young woman. I *need* sex. Will you see a doctor?"

The waitress brought their eggplant. As she turned away, Kurt picked up his fork and nodded. "Let's give it a couple of weeks. If things don't improve, I promise I'll see a doctor."

"But—"

"I've been feeling guilty; that may be part of it. And then the last couple of weeks we've been fighting. That may be part of what's behind it. Give it two weeks, Libby."

She felt suddenly tired and sad. "All right," she said, looking across the table at the lined face of her husband. Robert, she thought, trying hard to push the thought from her mind before it reached consciousness. Robert. What I need is a young man, vigorous, attracted to me, with all the years ahead of him that

I have. She felt her face grow warm and she lowered her eyes to her plate. "All right. Two weeks," she said and brought her fork to her mouth. For two weeks she would stay away from Robert. If Kurt could try, so could she.

That night Kurt came to Libby for sex, and for the first time she found that it was she who was ambivalent. She wondered if what had happened since their noontime conversation was responsible.

She had left their lunch longing to speak to her mother, to explain that things were working out for her and Kurt, that they had talked, that he was not unfaithful and would no longer see the other woman. Why it was so important that she see Alicia she wasn't sure, but it was a powerful need. She would have to wait till three-thirty when her mother returned from school.

The sitter she had arranged for was still with the children, so she spent the extra hours shopping for herself and the girls. Piling the colorful department store bags into the car, she made for the freeway. Now why, she asked herself as she pulled off at her mother's exit, all this urgency? Am I still working for my mother's approval? If so, why did I tell her about Kurt in the first place? And why didn't I suggest that she meet me downtown for coffee; she'd have liked that. It can't be that I want to see Robert; he'll be working. Do I just want proximity with him, his things, his house? The thought disturbed her.

But Robert was not at work. His car preceded hers along the winding road and he turned into his carport. As she pulled up, he hailed her distractedly. "I saw you back there. It's been a hell of a day," he said. "I'm due someplace momentarily and I had to stop to pick up something from the printer and"—he glanced at his wristwatch—"what the hell; I have a few minutes. Come on in."

She looked toward her mother's house. No rustle of blinds. "I'm just running by Mother's for a minute. Don't let me hold you up."

190

He waved her in. "You won't. I have to catch my breath before I leave." But halfway across the little living room he turned, blocking her further entrance. "What's happening with you, Libby? I hear you picked Kurt up for lunch today. Did you get this Nora thing straightened out?"

Her face grew warm. "I should never have told you." He was standing too close to her. She did not move. "We talked today."

"And?"

"He insists nothing happened between them. I—it seems so damned silly to be so disturbed over something like that. I mean these things happen every day. I'm attracted to other men; why shouldn't he be to other women?"

Robert placed a tentative finger under her chin and tipped it up. "How can you be twenty-eight? You look about ten right now. You find yourself attracted to other men?"

"Yes." She found it hard to breathe.

"I'm attracted, too." He swayed toward her and then, with a rough movement, turned away. "No."

"No?" She did sound like a child.

He was abruptly remote. "You'd better get on over to your mother's before—anyway, I have to leave."

She turned away, feeling empty. "Robert." She turned back. "Maybe—"

"No," he said harshly.

Afterward, telling her mother about Kurt and herself, she saw him leave the house. He looked as though he were in a hurry. When he had gone, she turned back to Alicia. "Oh, Mother," she said and burst into tears.

It was five-thirty before she had manufactured an explanation for her tears, done away with their traces and finally made her way home. Kurt had just walked in and was paying the sitter. Libby was all apologies to the girl.

The sitter was unruffled. "It's okay. It's fine. Really. I can use the extra money. And they were good, both of them."

"Where in God's name were you till this hour? It's nearly six. When I got in I imagined all sorts of things, the car in a ditch—"

"I ran over to Mother's. She seemed to need me." As she settled the girls before the television she thought, what a liar. It wasn't her mother who was needy. Or upset.

She came back into the kitchen. "She's all right now?" Kurt asked.

"Oh, yes." She began taking things from the refrigerator. "You know Alicia. She bounces back."

Kurt came up behind her and clasped his arms around her. "Did you tell her things were all right between us again?"

"Are they, Kurt?" She tipped her head back and looked at him. "I told her they were, in any case." She wriggled free and began mixing herbs into the ground beef. "Get out an onion, will you? Oh, God, there's the phone."

It was Ruth. "Libby, he did it!"

"Who did what?" Ruth did call at inconvenient times.

"Joel! He's sold the film—it's been picked up for distribution."

"Oh, that's different. That's wonderful!"

Kurt was signaling with raised eyebrows, waving the onion. "Of course—"

"Yes?" Libby nodded to him.

"It isn't over. That is, he apologized for not letting me know, for just going off all weekend, but he didn't seem—I don't know."

"What? Wasn't he happy?"

"His behavior was—puzzling. He seemed upset. And he looked *exhausted*. By the time he'd had a drink, he looked better. He told me not to mind him, he was just a moody artist and he'd better go off by himself. I had dinner all ready but he didn't even stay for that. You know, Lib, on an everyday basis, I think Joel would be hard to live with."

"Ruth, your news is wonderful, but I'm in the middle of getting dinner ready and the kids are starving."

"I'm sorry. I didn't think. He has something on his mind, that's all. He doesn't act the way a man—well, a man who's finally achieved what he's been working for so long should." Libby shifted the phone to her shoulder and took the onion from Kurt. "I'm sorry. I'll call later. Sorry I interrupted things."

Libby relented. "You didn't interrupt anything so urgent. Don't worry, Ruth—it's probably just letdown; you know how it is when you finally get something you've been wanting. You stand there with it in your hands and think, 'Was it all about *this*?'"

"What now?" Kurt said, as she put down the receiver.

"Joel's found a distributor." She picked up the knife. "Ruth thinks something's wrong, though."

"She's been in a stew for several days, hasn't she? It probably isn't anything."

"Probably not. Isn't that good news, though?"

"I knew he'd find someone. You know," he said, his voice wistful, "I haven't helped in the kitchen in a long time."

She laughed. "No, you're spoiled rotten. I always said you were." But she couldn't strike quite the note she sought; Robert's dark, intense face kept coming between her and her attempts. Thinking of that moment when he had moved toward her, she ran her tongue over her lips.

"You're quiet tonight," Kurt remarked. "Are you worried about Alicia?"

"No, not really, I guess I'm tired from my day away from home." But he kept his eyes on her, thoughtful.

It was not Kurt's night to supervise baths, but he volunteered. "Put your feet up and relax. I don't want you all tired out at bedtime. I have plans for us."

The thing for which she had been longing, Kurt's return to her, failed to please her. God, she thought as she undressed for bed, with Kurt watching from the other side of the room, am I going to have to pretend he's Robert in order to respond? Her reaction struck her as sad, as though Kurt's defection of the past two months had irrevocably marred something between them. Maybe they could no longer return to what they had.

The sex was unsatisfactory. On Kurt's part, despite his gaiety during the evening, it seemed labored, dutiful, and despite herself, she found she was visualizing Robert in his place, his artist's hands, his mouth, his dark eyes. Guilt kept her from complete immersion in the fantasy, and at the end she moved away from Kurt frustrated. Kurt knew; she could tell by his stillness as he lay on his side of the bed, unrelaxed.

She turned toward him and let one arm slide across his body. "It's been a while. I guess it takes time."

He laughed bitterly. "I'm out of practice?"

"Better than that you're in practice with someone else." But it crossed her mind, as she turned on her side away from him, that his problem might have been unfamiliarity. Had another body's contours become better known to him? Trust was hard to come by. She sighed softly and gave herself up to thinking about Robert.

44

"Do you realize," said Freda, "that we never see each other except at meals?" She had come downtown to meet him for lunch.

Pedersen laughed. "Is that an original way of saying we have to stop meeting like this?"

"It must be. It's true, though."

"Oh, not completely." He smiled. "I can think of a couple of other places where we see each other."

"Well, *that.*" She looked at him more closely. "Something's bothering you, Carl."

"It is." He picked up his fork. "I'm worried about that girl. Meredith. She's been seen twice—in fact, I caught a glimpse of her once myself—with a man who answers the description of the man seen with Lisa. I've warned her and I've tried to get her to name her friend, the man, but she refuses to pay any attention. I told you last night about the woman at the pool thinking she saw her."

"Yes. What about her?"

"Ron and I took that woman to the magazine, to *Intermission*, today to see if anyone looked familiar to her. We had to be pretty devious about it. We said she was working with us and left her standing to one end of the offices while we asked around, supposedly to see whether anyone had remembered anything further that he kids had said. We gave the woman a chance to get a good look, front and rear view—believe me, that took some maneuvering. But she said no one looked familiar. I don't know that I can trust that—different setting, distractions, no outdoor clothing. But it was a try. We tried her on Joel Sterne, too. No luck."

"Can't you have the girl followed?"

"How would anybody keep track of her at school? We have an appointment with her mother after lunch. I should have spoken to her before now."

"You should, Carl. It's not like you to wait like this."

"Until yesterday I wasn't that sure. Then when I phoned last night, the mother was out and this morning she wasn't at the magazine. She'll be in at two—we're going to talk then."

Freda was silent.

"It's all right. We'll find out who he is."

"You sound awfully sure."

"I am sure. I'm going to find out who her friend is, whether or not he's the man we're looking for. If we keep after the girl long enough, she'll tell us." He wished he felt as sure as he sounded.

Pedersen and Tate arrived at the *Intermission* offices at a quarter of two. Nora Crane was already there, waiting for them in the outer office.

Pedersen took in her appearance once again. She was small, a dark-haired woman, young looking to be the mother of a teenager, with a quick, intelligent face. Now concern was written across it. "What is it, Detective?" she said, addressing Pedersen. She ushered the two men away from the reception desk to a corner. "Something further on Lisa?"

"No." Pedersen leaned against a wall and looked at her. "This time it's about Meredith."

Alarm shot across her face. "What? Nothing's happened to Meredith?"

"No, no." He waited a moment till she calmed. "But I'm concerned that something may happen to her. Do you know"—he paused, searching for the right words—"if she has a man friend?"

"A *man* friend." Nora looked at them in disbelief. "Meredith? She hasn't even got a *boy*friend yet." She looked relieved.

"I think you may be wrong."

"This may be perfectly innocent, a family friend, an uncle," put in Tate.

"Yes," said Pedersen. "But we had to be sure."

She turned to Tate in appeal. "What is he talking about?"

Tate smiled at her. "Listen to him. You'll understand."

"Yes. Listen carefully. You may be able to straighten all this out in a minute. I saw Meredith biking—actually I saw her saying good-bye to a man and then getting on her bike—down on Cliff Drive last Saturday. Later that day I came by to see her. She wouldn't tell me his name. I accepted that, more or less, but I warned her that she should be careful, that Lisa was believed to have been with just such a man before her death." He could see how upset and uncomprehending she was. "It isn't just that. Meredith was seen by someone yesterday. In Richards West Park. She'd said she wouldn't see him again."

Fear darted in her eyes. "Richards West? I should think she'd be scared to go near the place."

"She was, by coincidence, seen in almost the same situation, saying good-bye to a man before she mounted her bike."

"It can't have been Meredith. She was home—well, actually it was five before she came in, but . . ."

"It was a girl with red hair. Meredith's appearance is distinctive."

"And the girl you—"

"Red hair, yes."

"I—I really don't know what to say. Meredith has no uncles that live here. We have no family friends who—" She paused.

"Well, none that has anything to do with her. One friend drops in now and then, but Meredith actively dislikes him. And she's such a little girl in those ways. I know she's twelve and she's quite mature in many senses, but when it comes to—well, really, she's much younger." Her face was white. "I'll talk to her as soon as she gets in from school. I'll find out. Thank you for telling me—you should have come Saturday when you first saw her."

"I think maybe I should."

"We can't very well follow her," Tate put in. "We don't have the manpower and we'd never be able to keep track of her at school."

"Follow her—oh, *no.*" She looked appalled at the idea.

"Perhaps," Pedersen said, "her brother. He might know something."

"Sean?" Her face twisted. "Maybe you should follow *him.* No, I don't mean that. It's just that his companions are pretty unsavory, whereas Meredith's have been—I just can't believe this. Meredith with a man."

"It may be nothing, of course, but under the circumstances—"

"Of course. It needs to be looked into right away. Thank you, Detective."

Pedersen hesitated. "You'll get back to us? If this man is completely innocent in intent, he won't mind a few questions."

"Yes." He could see her mind had moved ahead to the encounter with Meredith. She took the card he offered. "I'll get back to you."

"And, perhaps,"—he turned back once more—"it would be better not to spread the word about this."

"You needn't worry. Only Meredith is going to hear from me." Pedersen didn't envy the girl the confrontation.

As he and Tate walked down the steep stairs from the magazine's office, Pedersen said, "Parents are all alike, aren't they? Trusting."

"Naïve, I'd say."

"Yes, innocent. Until it's too late."

"This time maybe it isn't."

They walked silently to their car.

198

Meredith knew as soon as she entered her room that someone had been in it. Immediately she went to her journal. There it was, safely at the bottom of the hamper, wrapped as she always wrapped it, with the panties folded exactly, just as she folded them. She returned it to its hiding place, her sense of relief enormous. But someone had been in there—the books on her desk had been moved, her dresser drawers stirred up, the contents of her desk drawers rumpled. Someone had looked for the journal and not found it. For a moment, she had the frightening thought that it had been the detective, but he would never have broken into the house. It could only have been Sean. That thought was almost as frightening.

She sat down at her desk to think. Almost immediately she heard the door of the apartment close. She looked at the clock. Too early for her mother. It must be Sean.

A sharp knock startled her. The door opened and her mother was there, her mother with a strange expression on her face. She was still wearing her outside jacket.

"Meredith," she said, and immediately Meredith knew what was coming. She felt herself tremble.

"Yes?"

"I was visited by the police today."

"Mr. Pedersen."

"Yes, Detective Pedersen. Meredith, who is this man you've been seen with?"

Meredith made her eyes wide. "I don't know what he's talking about, honestly I don't. He came to see me, too. I think he has some other girl with red hair mixed up with me."

Nora Crane seated herself on the edge of the bed. "Meredith," she said, and then altered her tone. "Sweetie, there's a murderer out there, a man who killed Lisa, your best friend. It's not some crazy idea of mine, not just me being a pesty mother again. This is a *killer.*"

Meredith winced. "I know."

"Lisa's killer."

"I *know.* Don't keep saying it."

"You're meeting some man, Meredith, and I need to know who."

For one quavering moment, Meredith considered telling her mother everything—of the meeting, the misgivings, the renewed trust, everything. The idea of telling was delicious, not to carry the burden of deciding, of choosing, all by herself. Her mother would know what was right. Then she thought, But he isn't a murderer. If I tell her, she'll think he is, she'll go and tell that Pedersen detective and he'll make trouble, and then HE'll never have anything to do with me again. His face with the smile like her father's came into her mind. I can't do that to him, I can't. "I'm not meeting anybody. Really."

Her mother's figure sagged. "Meredith, what happened to that journal you used to keep? The one Sean and I gave you?"

"*You* did it."

"I did what?" Her mother looked genuinely surprised.

"You looked for it in my room?"

"No. I just got home; how could I have?" Something about the quirk of her eyebrows made Meredith wonder. Maybe we're both lying, she thought. "But," her mother went on, I'd be"—she chose the word carefully—"grateful if you'd—share it with me. It would make me feel surer, safer, that is, about you."

Meredith was shocked. "You told me that it was for my private thoughts and that no one else would see it."

"I know." Her mother's voice was weary. "I know I did, and I'm not violating your privacy. I'm *asking* you, Meredith, to share it with me. For safety's sake, your safety."

"You don't have any right. I'll tear it up, but I won't go showing it to anyone."

"You needn't destroy it, Meredith, and it's not everyone you'd be showing it to. Darling, do you think I want to come home one day and find you gone and then have you turn up in some bushes, maybe raped and strangled like Lisa? Do you think I want that?"

Meredith began to cry. "You keep saying those awful things to me. I'm not doing anything bad."

"I know." Her mother came over and put her arms around the girl. "I don't think you're doing anything bad. Just, maybe, dangerous. I'm trying to protect you."

All right, thought Meredith, in a sudden spurt of self-sacrifice. I'll make them all happy. I'll be miserable, but they'll be happy. I won't see him anymore. Just that one time Saturday and then I'll tell him I think my mother knows and doesn't like it. Her spirits plummeted at the thought of a final meeting. "All right," she said slowly. "I don't want to show you my journal, but I'll tell you everybody I go anyplace with. *Everybody.*" Except on Saturday, she thought, crossing her fingers of the hand her mother couldn't see. "Will that be better?"

"Yes." Her mother's eyes filled. "Oh, Meredith, that will be much better. I don't want anything to happen to you."

"Me neither," said Meredith. "I don't want anything to happen to me." After Saturday, she thought, I'll keep my promise. "Even if that detective did mix me up with some other red-haired girl."

Her mother looked at her. She wants to believe me, Meredith thought. Poor Mother. With a certain sadness, she reached out and patted her mother's hand.

45

Kurt had been peculiar about the dinner invitation to Syd. On the one hand, he seemed rather pleased that Libby had issued it; he liked Syd. But he found it hard to believe she had not even checked with him, Kurt. "What if I'd been tied up? Did you think of that?"

"On a Friday night? Why on earth would you be tied up?" She refused any longer to acknowledge that anything other than work should occupy him.

"Well. What time did you ask him for? The kids—"

"Eight. They'll be asleep."

"And he called to apologize?"

"Yes. He said he had behaved badly. He seems like a nice man, Kurt, just awfully—withdrawn or something. Funny, when he's so wonderful looking. You'd think he'd be full of himself."

Kurt had grunted, whether at her comment on Syd's good looks or at her saying the man was withdrawn, she did not know. Kurt was becoming as hard to read as Syd.

Thinking about all this as she put finishing touches to the

Friday night dinner—Kurt was upstairs reading to Katy—she decided they had really gotten nowhere with what she had come to think of as their problem. Kurt was no longer acting like a rebellious child, *showing* her, but something else, a quiet troubled something, edged through from time to time. As though he had something worrying on his mind. Well. In his own good time he'd tell her, no doubt.

Syd was prompt. He observes all the amenities, noted Libby, as he handed her a bottle of chilled wine. Funny that he comes across the way he does, being such a proper man.

"Kurt's tucking Katy in," Libby said, leading him into the living room. "He'll be right down. Would you like a drink?"

Once she had supplied him with bourbon and water, she excused herself to go to the kitchen. "I have to keep an eye out," she explained. "We don't want charred *boeuf Bourguignon.*"

"Horrors, no. Or should I say *horreurs?*"

She laughed. It was comforting to know the man had a sense of humor, even if it wasn't exercised very often.

Checking on the stew, she stopped to sip her own drink. She needed it; she had a feeling this evening would be rough going. With relief, she heard Kurt come down the stairs and greet their guest. Within minutes they were discussing the magazine. She relaxed as she took out the olives and artichokes to add to the salad.

Halfway through the evening she wondered if, no matter how long she knew him, she would ever feel close to Syd. It was as though he presented an armor, a tough shell to the world. She wondered what experience had made him like that.

"You said you had been married, Syd," she commented, aware that she might be treading into quicksand. "Was that recently?"

"No," he said.

"Oh, when you were a kid. I suppose I shouldn't speak that way of people in their twenties—I'm still in mine—but I feel infinitely older than anyone my age."

"Comes of living with an old man," Kurt remarked.

"I doubt that," Syd said. "Yes, I was in my twenties—early. It didn't last long." The alcohol seemed to have loosened his tongue. "Some men were never meant to be married."

"I think none of us was—with apologizes to you, Libby," Kurt said. "That, you realize, is a philosophic generalization, not a personal statement."

"Oh, absolutely," she said. "By the same token, *no one* was meant to be married. It's a queer arrangement all 'round."

Syd laughed. "I found it so."

She was thoughtful. "I'd have missed having a family, though—kids."

Kurt threw an unappreciative glance her way.

"I mean—I envy people like you, who seem to have the best of the single life. But kids are pretty important to me."

"I like children," Syd said.

"Does your own family—do your sisters and brothers and parents live here?"

"No." He lapsed back into taciturnity.

"Well, I'd better think about coffee and dessert." Libby took refuge in the kitchen. God, she thought, this is awful. What was I thinking of, inviting him? If I ever have him here again, I'll buffer us well with other guests. Garrulous ones.

Yet as soon as she was out of the room, she could hear the men begin to talk easily, sliding into comfortable shoptalk, laughing, in general behaving as anyone else did. It's me, she decided, it's because I keep wandering into forbidden topics. Yet she knew why she did it—it was an effort to break through to the real person, to hit some emotional lode in the man. If it's there at all, it's buried too deep for me to unearth, she decided. I'll have to settle for chitchat.

But when she returned to the table, she found herself once more moving into a subject that might lead to some revelation of the man. "Do you read a lot, Syd?"

"Quite a bit. When I'm home."

"You have favorite authors?"

"No, none in particular. I like Doctorow. Matthiessen. I have queer tastes, pretty eclectic."

"I loved *At Play in the Fields of the Lord*," Libby offered.

"I did, too. That wonderful conclusion."

So that's how he sees himself, Libby thought. He's something of a mystic. That's why I'm having such trouble with him. "I imagine you like Hesse," she guessed.

"Haven't read him. Should I?" He seemed to feel safe enough on this ground.

"Maybe *Siddhartha*. I haven't read it. But it's mystical, and you like that."

"I do?" He looked surprised.

"Well, I deduced you did—from the ending of the Matthiessen book."

"Oh, I suppose that was mystical. It doesn't mean I am."

"Of course not." Uncomfortably, she changed the subject. "How'd you ever get into advertising?"

"I don't know. By chance as much as anything. And then your husband convinced me *Intermission* needed me." He grinned at Kurt. "I figured I might as well starve in a good cause."

"I say—" Kurt began.

"I wasn't making a hell of a lot more before. This town doesn't have any Young and Rubicams. I'm not complaining."

Kurt sat back, uneasy.

"Did you study advertising?" Maybe he thinks I'm rude, she reflected. But he could ask us questions, too, she thought. How else do people get to know each other? But then again, she thought, he may just not be interested enough to want to get to know us; he may be totally self-absorbed.

"No, I don't have an M.B.A. or any courses in merchandising or advertising. I wasn't exaggerating. I fell into advertising by chance. Selling advertising space is not a high skill."

"The way you do it, it is," Kurt said. "This guy," he explained to Libby, "could sell a refrigerator to an Eskimo."

Syd laughed. "Well, not quite. It's not really very hard. Most people want to support *Intermission*. It's a bargain for them, an ad that goes into every house in the county."

"It's not all that much of a favorite. Now that we're going to be charging for it, we'll see how popular it is. And if that goes well, we may even be able to take you out of starvation status."

"It's not that important. I have simple tastes. Despite them, I loved your dinner, Libby."

She felt properly stroked. "Good. Let's take our coffee into the living room." Suddenly she wanted to move the evening along, get rid of Syd. His secretiveness, his lack of interest in others brought to mind someone squatting in a dank cave, sheltering there. In that moment she recognized that she would not only never really know him, but she would never really like him.

46

The week had dragged for everyone.

Libby, who did not go near her mother's nor Robert's, found the days until the weekend long and empty. Even the demands of the children's lives, a birthday party for Cory and a Parents' Day for Kate, did not relieve the sense of waiting. Kurt was attentive, loving, came home from work immediately after the magazine offices closed down. That didn't help.

And she gathered Ruth had heard nothing from Joel since that Wednesday visit. He had retreated back into silence. No one answered his phone.

For Meredith, increasingly apprehensive about the effect of her rejection on her friend, the time passed slowest of all. Her menstrual period had arrived on time and she had suffered only one day of mild discomfort this time. Maybe, as her mother had said, she had relaxed about it. She had not relaxed about anything else.

The time to the weekend seemed unbridgeable.

Friday evening Joel appeared as usual, his cheerfulness restored. Ruth hugged him hard. Later, however, telling Libby about their conversation, she sounded uneasy.

He was full of talk of the deal with Docufilm. "I can't stay over," he announced as he seated himself. "I have things to do. But I'll come by tomorrow night and stay over then."

She didn't let him see her disappointment. "Fine. I'll get things in for a good breakfast Sunday. We can sleep late and then contentedly stuff ourselves over the Sunday papers."

"Good." He seemed distracted.

"Are you—is whatever bothered you the other evening all right now?"

"What? Oh, yes. I was just tired. I'm fine." But he seemed distant. She asked no more questions.

"I think Kurt and Libby are repairing things between them," she remarked over dessert.

"Did things need repairing?"

"You remember. I told you about the Nora Crane business."

"Oh, that."

"Anyway, Libby talked with him and they agreed to give it a little time. You know,"—she paused, wondering whether to mention it—"I think Libby has a little crush on Robert Carter. He's the art director, I think it's called, at Kurt's magazine."

"A *crush*?"

She flushed. "Well, that does sound a little adolescent. She's attracted to him. He's a good-looking man. And nice, I gather."

"That won't help her and Kurt cure things between them."

"Oh, I don't think Kurt knows. She sees Robert when she visits her mother. He lives next door."

"Sounds complicated to me."

"If Kurt hadn't behaved that way, she'd never have paid any attention to anyone else."

His lip curled. "He drove her into Robert's arms?"

"I don't think she's been in Robert's arms; it's all on a fantasy level. But I wasn't going to say that, anyway." Was I? she wondered. Was she telling him this as a warning? Don't toy with me or I'll find someone else.

Suddenly he smiled. His smile was wonderful; Ruth felt her irritation with him melt away. "Sounds as though I'm about to play devil's advocate. Actually, I think it's great that Kurt and Libby are patching things up. I'm all for the lovers of the world staying in love." He leaned across the table and took her hand. "I think this film business has gotten to me. I haven't been very pleasant lately, have I?"

"Well—"

"I'll mend my ways. I have decisions to make, all sorts of decisions, Ruth. Once I've made up my mind about a few things, I'll be a different man. Guaranteed."

"I don't want you to be a different man."

"Well, then, I'll be my old adorable self." He grinned again.

She had to settle for that. Promises, she thought as she said good-bye to him after dinner. He hadn't lingered to make love. Something was still bothering him—maybe those decisions, maybe something else—but she wasn't relying on promises; she wanted to see action. She went into her bedroom to get into a housecoat, preparatory to an evening of television.

Libby had not seen Robert since their brief encounter on Wednesday. She had avoided her mother's house since then and, she told herself, thrown herself into the matter of correcting things between her and her husband. Kurt was trying mightily, coming home early, making love to her. That there was an element of strain in their relationship didn't offset the fact that he was trying.

Trying. That's the trouble, she thought as she changed the beds. Saturday was her day for major tasks, laundry, beds, usually marketing. Kurt had once asked her why Saturday. "Can't you do those things during the week and leave your weekends free for us? For the family?" For a brief time she had revised her schedule, but Kurt was away so often on Saturdays that finally she had returned to her old way of doing things.

Today, for example, he was away. He had assured her that it was necessary and had nothing to do with Nora Crane, and she had believed him. He promised to be back by four to take the kids for a couple of hours. She wondered vaguely what was so important he had to do it on a Saturday, but she hadn't asked and, since the switchboard was closed down weekends, she couldn't reach him to see if he was indeed at work. Really, she didn't care; that was the disturbing fact. Something had happened in her relationship with Kurt, a subtle shift that had realigned things between them. The caring, which she had felt so intensely for a while, was simply not there any longer. She stood for a moment, the clean sheet not yet unfolded, wondering what sort of future they would have without caring.

Now what to do with the rest of the day, she thought as she mitered the last corner and pulled the spread over the bed. I could take the kids and drop in on Mother. Not to see Robert, but really to see Mother.

Rounding up some things for them to play with—a coloring book and crayons, a ball, two dolls—she decided that she'd take lunch along. Phoning Alicia, she arranged to stop at a deli; her mother promised coffee, and fresh-baked cookies for the little girls. Libby took out a couple of sweaters, gathered up the girls and piled them into the car.

Robert's house was silent, blinds drawn. Leaning forward, she peered into his carport. He was out. His car was gone. Good, she told herself, I won't have the discomfort of wanting to go next door, wanting to be with him. Besides, she reminded herself, he said no to me, he doesn't *want* us to be involved. She sat for a minute in the car until the emotion she was feeling subsided, then she opened the doors for the girls.

Alicia greeted them with grandmotherly warmth, tossing a canny glance at Libby. She knows, Libby thought, she knows. She's figured out what that outburst of mine on Wednesday was all about; she wasn't fooled when I said it was just relief that things were straightening out between Kurt and me.

Ringing a platter with the moist pink cold cuts and scooping the creamy delicatessen potato salad into a bowl, she thought, They look delicious; love hasn't affected my appetite. And she realized she had for the first time named her feeling.

Meredith had not slept all night. Perhaps a bit toward morning, but really, she thought, not all night. She woke from an exhausted early morning doze to the sun shining brightly in her window. It was going to be a glorious day.

During the sleeplessness of her night, she had worked and worked over how she would handle today's visit. First, time for ordinary visiting, so she would at least have that. Then time for serious talk, for her explanation that she was sure her mother suspected she was seeing someone older. Or should she tell him immediately; was it unfair to him to go on as usual without telling him? Then she pulled herself up short: did it *matter* to him? He was just being kind, an adult humoring a child—well, a young girl. Would it really matter to him that she could no longer meet him? Yet something told her it would matter.

And should she tell him her mother actually knew, all but his name? If she were to keep her promise, she would have to be definite in what she was saying. Perhaps, she thought as she turned her pillow for the fourth time, it would be better just to let whatever happened happen naturally. Maybe the subject of their meetings would come up of themselves.

This is what I get, she thought irritably, catching a glimpse of the dial on her bedside clock and noting that it was already eight. But, she reasoned, he suggested the meetings, even the first glass of iced tea. He's grown-up and he doesn't know any better, either. She sighed and climbed out of bed. Really, it was a hopeless situation.

She dressed with care, putting on a denim skirt so infrequently worn that it was still stiff with newness. At breakfast, Sean looked at her with interest. "Dressed up?" he asked. Meredith scowled into her cereal bowl. "No, I'm not dressed up," she said.

Her mother roused herself from the morning paper. "You do look very nice, Meredith. I'm glad to see you're finally wearing that skirt. Are you doing something special today?"

"No." Meredith was amazed at how casual her voice sounded. "I'm just tired of jeans. I thought after the washing I'd go by and see if Jennie wants to take a walk."

Her mother looked at her thoughtfully and then returned to her newspaper.

"You haven't seen much of Jennie lately, have you?" Sean asked. It seemed an idle inquiry, but Meredith knew him too well to assume any inquiry Sean made was idle. "Pretty much," she said. "She dances almost every afternoon."

"She's really going to be a ballet dancer?" The idea apparently amused him.

"Yes. What are you going to be? A drug dealer?"

Her mother, half listening, said, "Meredith!"

Sean smiled the strange smile he so often gave her. "You don't think I'd tell you? If I knew, that is."

"I'm your sister," said Meredith, sweetly reasonable.

"You sure are." She had quieted Sean. He returned to his breakfast, no longer interested in what she was wearing or what friend she planned to see.

Helping her mother clear the table, she prepared the way for an early departure. "I think I'll sort the laundry now. Maybe Jennie and I can have lunch out." She was mildly shocked at the ease with which lies were rolling from her tongue today.

"You have enough money?"

"Yes." She went into her room and began emptying the hamper. This lying might be easy, but it did not feel good.

When the laundry was tumbling in the washer, she returned to her room and took out her journal, exposed now that it was not embedded in soiled clothes. She sat down at her desk.

Saturday, April 23

He went to my mother! *That Mr. Pedersen—Detective Pedersen, I guess I'm supposed to call him. He told her he'd seen me and then somebody else saw me with a man and had her all scared and worried.* Honestly! *Finally she made me promise I wouldn't see HIM anymore—no, that's not what she made me promise, because I told her he had me mixed up with some other red-headed girl. What she made me promise is that I won't go anyplace or with anyone without telling her. I said I wouldn't, but I crossed my fingers so I didn't have to tell her I'm going to see him once more and tell him.*

I'm not sure just what I will tell him—that Mother's heard I was seeing someone, but she doesn't know who, I guess. After all, I promised him it would be our secret, although with all the people around town who have seen us, it doesn't seem like much of a secret.

But I feel bad. I like him. It's been like having Daddy back and I felt sort of taken care of and—loved, I guess. My mother is fine and even Sean's okay sometimes, but I miss Daddy. I never say anything about it, but I think about it a lot. A lot. And I'm not sure what HE's going to think. One thing, he'll think I'm such a little girl that I have to do just what my mother says. Maybe he'll be mad at me, too. I wouldn't like him to be mad at me. After all, pretty soon I'll be older and won't have to do exactly what my mother says. Maybe then—well, I won't think about that now.

It depresses me to write all this. I guess I'll go see what the laundry's doing. We're meeting at the university library, downstairs in that pretty patio. I don't want to keep him waiting.

47

Saturday morning in the Pedersen household was errand time. Freda had taken the marketing, Carl Pedersen the odds and ends.

"Now please don't forget that poster board, Carl," she reminded him as he picked up the list and started toward the door. Freda's duties with the civic theater group, The Players, were multifold.

"It's on the list?"

"Yes, the size and weight. White is fine."

Later, in Palmer's Stationery he stood waiting for his purchases to be rung up. The store was known for its continuing sales. Today everything in sight seemed to be on sale: on the counter alone boxes of felt pens, gum erasers, white-out, camel's hair brushes, memo pads, bond paper, diaries. He idly rummaged through them while he waited, deciding he could use a couple of black pens. Then, with a suddenness that startled everyone, he dropped the pens and the sheets of poster board and bolted from the store.

214

The clerk gazed after him. "Did he steal something?"

One of the customers laughed. "No, he's a cop; I recognize him. Maybe he saw a criminal go by the store."

They stood staring after the hastily retreating figure, shaking their heads. The clerk picked up the poster board and straightened a bent corner.

Outside, Pedersen was heading for his car.

At the Ash Street apartment, he parked in a no-parking zone. Mrs. Crane had just come in; she was unloading a filled market cart.

He was still breathless. "Mrs. Crane," he said. "Your daughter has a journal."

She looked puzzled. "Yes. Did she tell you?"

"No. Talk about slow on the uptake. Way back early in the investigation, someone told me your daughter thought of herself as Anne Frank. I was standing in a stationery store today and I looked down at a stack of diaries and—"

"You realized what that meant."

"Yes."

She smiled. "She never told me she identified with Anne Frank." The smile faded. "Are you asking to see her journal?"

"I think I must."

Nora Crane hesitated. "I told her it would be hers, completely private."

"You want her around to make entries in it." His voice was gentle.

She looked at him, frightened.

"Do you know where it is?"

"No. We could look." She led him into Meredith's bedroom.

Pedersen found it right away. "It's actually a rather common hiding place for journals, although Meredith wouldn't know that." He riffled through the pages, checking the last few days. "Thank God she's candid."

"What?" Her mother looked at the book in his hands. "Oh, my God. She's meeting him—right now."

"Yes, but she says where. What time did she leave? Did she leave around eleven, do you know?"

"She must have, or eleven-thirty. I wasn't here. Are you going to do something—can you find her? You *have* to find her, Detective Pedersen. Trails—Lord, there must be dozens of trails on campus."

"We'll start looking. I need to use your phone."

Ron Tate was at home. Pedersen explained. "We've got to get over there. It's noon now"—he checked his watch—"closer to twelve-fifteen. Meet me at the university library, in front."

He turned to Mrs. Crane. "Don't worry. We'll find her. Meanwhile, I think you might be wise to violate your daughter's privacy and find out what this is all about."

48

He was waiting in the shadowy well of the library patio; she walked through the library and down the stairs to meet him. He had on jeans and a backpack, which made her smile. "Is that our lunch?"

He nodded. He looked happy, she noticed with a twinge. "Come on," he said. "There are some wonderful trails back here. Are you starved?"

She was, but she was embarrassed to mention it, so she shook her head. These days she was always starved; she must be growing or something.

Surprisingly, the paths were empty of people. "Doesn't anyone else know about these trails?" she asked.

He laughed. "Quite a few people. We're just in luck today." He looked at her. "You look very nice. You don't often wear a skirt, do you?"

"I used to hate to wear anything but jeans, but I'm beginning to like wearing skirts." She couldn't tell him she had dressed up for the occasion of giving him her bad news.

The day was brilliant. Sunlight filtered through the branches; beyond the sky was cloudless. "It's like summer, isn't it?" she said wistfully.

"Yes, but don't cry about it." He smiled and her heart turned over. How was she ever going to tell him?

They selected a place off the path under a redwood for lunch. Occasional cracklings among the twigs suggested that there were passersby, but none came into view. "This is *great*," she said.

He opened the backpack. "See," he said, unwrapping a sandwich and flipping back the top slice of bread. "Ham. The perfect accompaniment to pickles." The fat rosy slices of ham against the thick wedges of bakery bread looked delicious; she swallowed, her appetite gone. He opened a little plastic container jammed with pickles, dill and sweet. "Didn't know exactly what you meant by pickles. There's mustard if you want it; I didn't put anything on the sandwiches. And one more thing." He turned to her. "Do you drink wine?"

"A little. My mother lets me with meals once in a while, mostly when there's company."

"Well,"—he took out a half-liter bottle—"we'll have a drop, just to celebrate this beautiful day. I even brought glasses." He fished out a pair of wine glasses and poured her glass a quarter full. "Just a drop. I wouldn't want you to do anything your mother wouldn't approve of." He filled his glass and touched it to hers. "To us. To lots of walks."

She drank and immediately felt the warmth of the unfamiliar liquid in her belly. How was she going to say it?

"Now," he said, "let's settle down and eat pickles to our heart's content. I like pickles, too," he confided.

She had to smile. In some ways he was as young as she.

After they had eaten, they continued to sit, he leaning against a tree, she near him cross-legged on the edge of the plastic tablecloth he had brought along.

She might as well do it. She had passed up a couple of natural openings; she was just stalling. She felt sad. "I have something to tell you," she said.

218

"Yes?" He poured himself a third glass of wine. "What's that?" He smiled, *that* smile.

"I don't know how to say it. My mother found out about us." That seemed an odd way to put it. "I mean she found out that I was meeting someone much older than me. She didn't like it."

He was silent, his face suddenly bleak.

"She doesn't know who you are"—she looked up at him in appeal—"I kept our secret, but she knows I'm seeing somebody. I lied and told her I wasn't, but I promised in the future I wouldn't go anywhere with anyone without telling her. Usually I don't lie. I have to keep my promise."

"You mean—"

Miserably she nodded. "I can't meet you anymore. I'm sorry."

"But—you can't *leave* me."

She was confused. "Leave you?"

"You can't *leave* me." The urgency in his voice increased. "You don't understand. It's too soon—I didn't mean to talk to you about it yet—but I love you."

She stared at him. Maybe he wasn't so grown-up.

Moving closer to her, he took her two hands in one of his. "You"—he said, and he ran his other hand over the contours of her face—"you just don't understand what you mean to me, Meredith. I love you. I *want* you."

She shrank back, unable to think of anything to say. As she tugged her hands to free them, his grip moved to her wrists and tightened. "Meredith," he said huskily, and suddenly his body was on hers and his hand was on her leg. His weight held her down; she could feel his hands crawling up under her skirt. She heard herself speak. "Lisa," she said, her voice hoarse.

"That was different. I didn't care for her. I—it was an accident, Meredith."

She gave one horrified shriek before he yanked one hand free and clapped it over her mouth. Lisa, she thought, you—Lisa. Oh, no, you did that to Lisa.

Then a streak of blue descended on them and she was suddenly freed. Her brother stood struggling with the man who had risen from the ground, looking around as though he were

219

dazed. Then the man was gone, tearing down the hill, nearly knocking over two men hurrying toward him.

Pedersen and Tate looked at each other. "That's him," Pedersen said and looked up the hill to where a boy and a girl stood together.

S ean put out a hand. "It's all right. It's all right." She was crying. "Cut it out. You're okay; he didn't have time to do anything to you." Awkwardly, he wiped her face with his hand.

She gulped. "How did you—"

"I followed you. I thought I'd starve while I watched you eat that lunch, but I stayed close."

"I didn't see you—"

"It's just a fucking good thing I was here. How you could be so stupid—" He broke off; she was still being shaken by sobs. "Stop blubbering, Meredith, you're *okay*."

"But, Sean, how did you know to—"

"I read your journal." He gave her an unpleasant smile. "All about your weird brother. Among other things." They began walking down the hill, backpack, tablecloth, wine bottle forgotten behind them. "When you changed the hiding place, I decided I'd better keep track. I figured you were up to something. That was a dumb place to put it. Anybody would've guessed." He laughed.

"It never looked as though—"

"I got smart after you wrote that I'd left traces the first time I read it. I left it just the way I found it. But I was fucking curious about who the guy was."

"Stop saying that."

"Oh." His mouth twisted. "You practically get yourself raped and you worry about my language."

"I didn't. I'd have—yelled or something."

"Listen. If I hadn't been there, you could have been lying strangled, like your girl friend."

"You're so awful to me." Her mouth trembled. "I don't see why you'd even want to save me."

"I couldn't let you be *raped*, could I?" His voice was grim.

"I think you're wonderful, Sean."

He stopped and looked at her. "Holy shit!" He shook his head. "Don't get carried away. I'm the same weirdo you wrote about in your diary."

"I don't care. I think you're wonderful."

He walked on, his back to her. "Where's your bike? Do you think you can get yourself home without getting into any other trouble?"

"Aren't you coming with me?"

He shrugged. "Why should I? You're okay." He strode off in the direction of his cycle.

Just beyond them, within earshot, the detectives looked at one another. Then they joined Meredith.

49

When it came out, when it was in the newspapers and everyone knew that a young art director named Robert Carter had been arrested for the attempted rape of a twelve-year-old girl and the murder of another, Libby at first denied it. It was a mistake, she insisted, some dreadful mistake. She couldn't tell anyone her reasoning, that Robert had refused to allow even a full-grown woman to seduce him.

And Nora Crane's daughter, that somehow made it more frightening and real, yet more incredible. The girl must have imagined the assault, or her brother had. Even Robert's eventual confession, his admitting to the killing of Lisa Margolin— an accident, he insisted—made without benefit of attorney, although his rights had been read to him, didn't convince her.

It took her a week to accept his guilt. During that week she wasn't so much angry at this mistake on everyone's part as depressed. As though she were mourning someone. She thought about it every day. Then it occurred to her that it was not someone but something she was grieving over. It was her romantic notion that something would evolve between them. Something that would have done away with the necessity, the arduous chore, of reestablishing a relationship with Kurt. Finally she recognized it was true: Robert Carter was a rapist, a murderer. A—it was hard even to think the word—a pedophile.

She and Kurt had discussed it when it first happened, when she was still in the it-must-be-a-tragic-misidentification phase. When, finally, she came to terms with the fact of Robert's— problem, they talked again.

The children had been put to bed, and they were sprawled, tired, in the living room having a drink, a rare activity for them at this time of day.

"It's been awful these last few weeks, hasn't it?" Libby remarked. She gathered herself into a little bundle in the corner of the sofa.

"It hasn't been easy," her husband agreed.

"This Robert Carter business and . . ." Her voice trailed off.

Kurt sat straighter in his chair and crossed his ankles. "You liked Robert Carter." It was a statement.

"I did. I never thought he'd do anything like that. He was such a good neighbor, sort of looking out for Mother. . . ."

"And you."

She too sat straighter. "What are you getting at?"

"I'm getting at something we should have talked about long before this. You were attracted to Robert Carter. Perhaps you even had something going with him?"

"The best defense is an offense. Is that going to be the next accusation?"

"Well, it's crossed my mind."

She looked down at her glass, as though she had forgotten she held it. "I was attracted to him. Nothing was going on."

"Not because you didn't want it to."

"Kurt." She looked at him with the first real candor in weeks. "It's all mixed up. I thought you were having an affair, I was vulnerable, I met Robert and he seemed to like me—it's all mixed up. Maybe even some getting even was involved."

"But he was interested only in little girls."

Pain crossed her face. "That's about the size of it."

"And I, who didn't really have an erotic thought—"

"You didn't? Then what the hell were you doing spending all that time at Nora Crane's?"

"I'll tell you." He leaned forward as though to draw closer to her. "It was to get away. From, not to. From demands. From needing to be home at a certain time. From having to bathe the kids every other evening and take them to the park every weekend and be a good father at all times. From your discontent."

"My discontent?" She was surprised.

"You aren't aware, you haven't named it, but you're bored and unhappy. You need to get away yourself, to work or school, to do something to get yourself out of this household rut. I was always conscious that you were staying home because you thought it was what I wanted."

"But it wasn't, Kurt. It was what I wanted, too, for now. I've been restless, sure, but I knew it wasn't going to last. I didn't realize I'd been—"

"Maybe I exaggerated it. But I felt that home had become a—an unhappy place. A place where I wanted to bury myself in television or a book or a newspaper. A place from which I wanted to escape."

"And Nora's home didn't have that feel."

He laughed. "Strangely enough, before I was through it did. *She* began to make demands, unstated but they were there. Maybe it's in the nature of relationships, any relationship. At first there was just this place where nothing was expected of me. She'd get me a drink, make me dinner, we'd sit and chat about work or about her kids. But eventually, the fact that I didn't make a pass bothered her. She felt it was some shortcoming on her part. And her son didn't like me, I couldn't help with him. Even her daughter disliked me at first, until Nora brought her and her friend up to the magazine for that visit. Then the kid began to see me as a writer—she wants to be a writer when she grows up. But in the end, I was glad to get out of the situation, to have a reason, an excuse for getting out."

"And that's why you came back to me. Because you were fed up with Nora's demands. Not for—me?"

"It was for you, too. I love you, Libby—should I say, in my fashion? I suppose the reason I didn't marry till so late was that I shouldn't have married at all. I don't do well boxed into a situation, a routine. I love you and I love the kids and, if you'll bear with me, I'll try to alter some of my attitudes. But you need to know it won't be easy and maybe I won't succeed. Maybe that's not enough for you, maybe you don't want to settle for half a loaf." He laughed. "I never thought I'd end up referring to myself as half a loaf. The other thing, Libby, is that I think you should go back to work. I think things will be vastly improved between us—or for you, if things don't work out for us—if you do that." He rose and went over to the sofa where she sat. "I've been honest. Maybe too honest. All the things you always wanted to know about Kurt but were afraid to ask?"

She huddled against him. "It sounds bleak."

"Not too. I love you. Do you love me?"

She tilted her face back. "I don't know, Kurt. I just don't know anymore."

"Shall we give it a go? See what happens? Give ourselves a deadline, a reasonable one, and see how things look then?"

"A deadline?" She laughed. "Ever the editor."

"For the kids' sake, at least. At Nora's I saw what divorce does to kids."

She glanced away. "I know all about that. I guess we should. No promises. Except"—she looked into his face—"that we'll both be faithful until the—deadline. I can't cope with worrying about that, too."

"I can't, either. And I think the likelihood of sexual adventure is far greater with you. I have my bachelorly ways. Sex doesn't excite me as much as it does you."

"You seem—lately you seem—"

"I'm learning. Again," he said. "You've been giving good instruction. Maybe I'll turn around and become the sex-crazed husband of the century."

"Who knows, my lessons are pretty potent." She laughed softly. "I think I do love you, Kurt. We'll give it that go." She stood up, taking his hand. "Till the deadline. Let's go practice."

Later, Libby learned that in Ruth's living room the conversation also centered on Robert Carter. "Did you ever meet him, Joel?" Ruth asked.

"I think once, when Nora Crane interviewed me. I'm not sure. The photograph in the paper didn't look too familiar."

"You know it was Nora Crane's daughter who was almost—"

"I know. Her I did meet. She and her friend, the one who was strangled, visited the magazine that day I was there. Two bright little girls, full of ideas about being writers someday."

"And now one is dead and the other probably traumatized."

"Maybe not. Her brother got there before anything really happened."

"But the first time she has sex, it'll all come back. How could she not be traumatized?"

"You're probably right." He looked at her. "Not to change the subject or anything, but I've been a bastard lately, haven't I?"

"Well . . . unpredictable, certainly."

He laughed. "And you're not going to ask why."

"I tried that. With poor results."

"Yes, you did. I'll tell you what's been bugging me, Ruth. I like us, our being together like this. I've wanted to ask you if you'd like to make it permanent, but this damned film business has fucked everything up. Then when I realized I'd better begin to job hunt someplace, someplace that certainly couldn't be Bay Cove, I realized I couldn't ask anything of you. To ask you to leave a job you've worked at for years, where you've moved ahead and have a decent income, to come and live on a shoestring or maybe no shoestring at all with me—how could I do that?"

"I thought—"

"I know, you thought I was losing interest. Didn't we once talk about how easy it is for women to think that?"

"But you—"

"I grant you I was being—what?" He paused, searching for a word.

"Enigmatic?"

He laughed and leaned over to hug her. "At least enigmatic."

"So where are we now?"

"That's my girl. It's the practical side of you I love best, Ruth. It's such a contrast to my head-in-the-clouds approach to things. Don't you think we'd make a terrific married couple?"

"If we had something to eat. An empty belly can do dreadful things to romance."

"I think I have the solution. And we won't have empty bellies."

"The Docufilm thing?"

"Yes. But not just *Bible Story*. They want me to do some treatments for them of other films; in fact, they're prepared to take me on full time."

"Oh, Joel. What will that do to your own work? Will that leave any time for filmmaking?"

"We're going to work something out so I'm on my own three months a year."

"They must really want you."

"They must. How does the whole idea grab you?"

"But if you're on full-time salary, where will you have to live?"

"For now I can stay here in Bay Cove, work out of my place. It'll mean hopping planes to go south regularly or driving down. You like long drives. But they're willing to try it on my terms, at least at first. How about you?"

"What do you mean?"

"Are you willing to try it on my terms? Marry me or shack up or whatever suits you, but be together?"

"Is this"—she smiled—"what in old-fashioned terms might be regarded as a proposal?"

"You've got my number. It is."

"Have you a ring?"

"As a matter of fact—" He poked in his pocket.

"Joel! You don't!"

"Well"—he grinned—"it's a temporary one. From inside a

cereal box, in fact. It said on the box, 'Beautiful ring with genuine stone enclosed.' I haven't eaten any of the cereal yet." He formally presented it.

"I accept. You don't think I'd let a gem like this slip through my fingers. It's"—she slipped it on one finger, then another—"a little large. What sort of child do you suppose this was made for? And what's the stone? It could be an opal."

"Never! Opals are bad luck. It's a diamond. It's just larger than you're used to your diamonds being."

She smiled and kissed him. "I think it's going to be fun being married to you. When you aren't being a bastard."

"Never," he said. "Never again. My bastardhood is over."

"**R**uth," said Libby. "That's wonderful. Although I'd hardly call it his bastardhood." She laughed. "This is such exciting news. You know, I'd begun to think there never would be any good news again."

"You feel bad about Robert. Don't, Lib. Feel good about yourself and Kurt."

"I'll try. Robert must be two different people. The man I knew—"

"Libby."

"You're right. I think things'll work out for Kurt and me. For everyone but the Margolins, things seem to have worked out. Those poor people."

"Yes," said Ruth. "Those poor people. I wonder what they're thinking now."

50

"It's sort of sad, isn't it?" Freda said.

It was a Saturday evening and they were seated in their favorite seafood restaurant at a window overlooking the water. It was the first dinner they had eaten out since Pedersen had started working on the Lisa Margolin death; it was in celebration of putting the case behind them.

He grinned. "You mean sad that I didn't accomplish more? And faster?"

"Of course I don't mean that." She sounded angry. "I mean that that artist did that, killed her. In the papers they said he swore it was an accident, that he was trying to quiet her and just—did it too hard."

"That's what he says. But how could he have let her go? She would have identified him."

"I know. Just the same, I hope it was an accident."

"Hard to believe, after a rape attempt." He picked up his napkin. "I certainly didn't pull off any grand moves in this case. We moved in, but without the brother, we might have another

229

case of strangulation on our hands. By the time we made it there, there wasn't much left but a half-empty bottle of wine and a container of pickles. And the girl walking down the hill with her brother."

"You set things in motion. You told the mother, you talked to her. That girl was not going to see him again."

"Except for that one last visit in a secluded spot. She didn't pay much attention to what I told her, did she? Freda, this is one for which I can't take a lot of credit." The waiter served their fish soup. "This looks marvelous."

"Mmm. You can't work miracles, Carl."

He smiled at her. "My most loyal fan. But I think it was more than working miracles. Much as I wanted to clear up this case, find the—bastard who'd done it, I was immobilized."

She looked at him.

"By my involvement."

"Your emotional involvement?" She lifted her spoon to her mouth. "God, this is good. I could make a whole meal of it."

"Yes, I couldn't think straight about this case. I promptly forgot that business of Anne Frank. If I'd got to that little girl's journal sooner—it wasn't till I stood at that stationery counter and looked down at those diaries that I thought of it. Remembered. And not until I glanced at those camel's hair brushes did it occur to me that the piece of bamboo we'd filed away could have come from an artist's paintbrush." He paused in his eating. "Jesus, I hate working on things that involve kids. And those two—that Lisa with her poems and her independence. And Meredith—red-headed Meredith." He laughed. "Poor kid, it was a little hard remaining anonymous with that hair."

"You talked to her afterwards?"

"Yes. She said Robert Carter *needed* to kill Lisa. When I pinned her down, she said he had told her one time that Lisa's killer did it out of a 'terrible necessity.' Or something like that."

"That's what it must have been, a terrible necessity. A man like that, an artist, a cultivated man—how dreadful for him to be obsessed that way."

"It is. Meredith said she thought it was her telling him she couldn't see him after they'd had such a pleasant time, the

230

walk and lunch—and he incidentally, had drunk quite a bit of his lunch—that caused him to go crazy that way. She said he kept saying she couldn't leave him."

"Poor kid, she probably hadn't a notion what it was all about."

"She said just as he threw himself on top of her, she thought, 'Lisa—he did do that to Lisa.' She's pretty smart."

"Smart, but she couldn't have had anything like that in her experience. Will she be all right?"

"I think so. She seems like a very sturdy kid. Resilient. Afterwards she talked a lot about her father, how he reminded her of her father. I think Meredith's mother and father have had several long talks since then, from what Mrs. Crane said. She told me Meredith's father was appalled at what had happened and plans to see a lot more of the two kids. Mrs. Crane told him some of what she found in the journal."

"Divorce. Why don't people stay together and try to work things out?"

"That's a good question. You wonder whether they do better on the second—and third try. I suspect they just haul along all the same garbage, the same problems. Maybe not."

"Think how many broken families there are now. How many single mothers trying to work and care for children."

"I know." After a moment he said, "I saw the Margolins. They wanted us to take them to visit Carter."

"How awful for them. Why would they want that? Did you take them?"

"It was awful. For them and for him. He broke down and wept, begged them to forgive him, swore he never meant to kill her or even to hurt her. They sat there as though they were encased in ice, unable to be moved by his tears. And the tears were hard to believe, even for me. I think the Margolins felt they might understand better after seeing him, but when they walked away they looked as sad and bewildered as before."

"Oh, Carl."

"You know, I think I understand why after he killed her, Carter took the time to pull up her jeans. I think he was trying to restore her, put her back the way she'd been. Make it not have happened. Yet in some way when the—obsession, the impulse took over, he became cold enough to assault a child."

"Did you ever find out how he got her to go with him?"

"They'd made friends, in a way. He was taken with her during that visit to *Intermission* and hung around her house off and on until he ran into her. When I asked how he had gotten her to go with him that day, he said he told her a child was in trouble and needed her help."

"How ironic. She was the child in trouble."

"Yes."

"Well, thank God Meredith's mother didn't have to go through what the Margolins did."

"Thank God is right. Oh, look at this." Their lobster had arrived. The waiter deferentially dropped a bib around her neck and then his.

"Let's not talk about it anymore," she said. "This is no way to enjoy lobster."

"Right," said Pedersen, picking up his nutcracker. "It's not."

51

Meredith took her journal from her desk drawer. She no longer had to hide it. She opened the book.

I don't even know what the date is. It's been such a crazy time. HE—Robert, I can say it now, but I don't even want to—is in jail. He killed Lisa and I guess he would have killed me. Every time I think of him putting his hand over my mouth that way, I start to shiver. When Lisa died, I felt funny for a long time. Sort of as though I was dead, too, inside. But this is worse.

But I remember once writing that when bad things happen, sometimes good ones do, too. Sean is just the same, awful to me—you'd think being treated like a hero would have improved him, but it didn't. But Daddy has been coming over—he was here three times this week. He's told us all about the baby and he does want us to visit after it's born, and he even apologized for that letter he dictated to his secretary. He said it was "insensitive." I don't know

233

how he knew it bothered me, but I guess he must have thought about it later. He says we're going to have a regular time every week to see him—one for me and one for Sean. Sean sort of sneered, but I think he was pleased—I don't know why I think that, but I do. Even if Daddy won't ever live with us again, I feel as though I've got my father back.

And my mother has a new boyfriend. They're pretty lovey-dovey, different from her and Kurt (he never comes over anymore), but I suppose he won't last long. They never do.

I'm tired tonight and I don't want to think about any of it. My mother had a lock put on my door that I can unlock with a key. That means at least I have my privacy, but I'd rather have the old unlocked door if none of this could have happened. Maybe when I see Daddy next time I'll feel better. I hope so.

She returned the journal to her desk drawer. She was feeling shivery again and all she wanted to do was get into bed. "Good night," she said aloud to no one in particular as she pulled the blankets up around her chin.